WORLD'S WORST TIME MACHINE

OTHER BOOKS BY DUSTIN BRADY

Escape from a Video Game: The Secret of Phantom Island
Escape from a Video Game: Mystery on the Starship Crusader
Escape from a Video Game: The Endgame
Trapped in a Video Game
Trapped in a Video Game: The Invisible Invasion
Trapped in a Video Game: Robots Revolt
Trapped in a Video Game: Return to Doom Island
Trapped in a Video Game: The Final Boss
Superhero for a Day
Leila & Nugget Mystery: Who Stole Mr. T?
Leila & Nugget Mystery: The Case With No Clues
Leila & Nugget Mystery: Bark at the Park

DUSTIN BRADY

Illustrated by Dave Bardin

Andrews McMeel
PUBLISHING®

Andrews McMeel Publishing
a division of Andrews McMeel Universal
1130 Walnut Street, Kansas City, Missouri 64106
www.andrewsmcmeel.com

23 24 25 26 27 SDB 10 9 8 7 6 5 4 3 2

ISBN Paperback: 978-1-5248-7708-8
ISBN Hardback: 978-1-5248-8413-0

Library of Congress Control Number: 2022948550

Photo credits: page 180, Fred Barker, Minnesota Historical Society;
page 181, Doc Barker, St. Paul Daily News, Minnesota Historical Society

Made by:
RR Donnelley (Guangdong) Printing Solutions Company Ltd.
Address and location of manufacturer:
No. 2, Minzhu Road, Daning, Humen Town,
Dongguan City, Guangdong Province, China 523930
2nd Printing—5/15/2023

CONTENTS

1   Race Against Time 1

2   The Mad Scientist Down the Street 7

3   Garage Sale of the Century 13

4   BYOC 21

5   World's Worst Time Machine .25

6   Tommy Twinkles 33

7   Cheetos 39

8   Chaos 45

9   Thomas Edison Robs a Bank .53

10   Plan D 61

11   Liam the Liar 69

12   Creepy Karpis and the Barker Boys 79

13   Home Alone 85

14   Frankenstein Santa 91

15   No Funny Business 101

16   Sweet Dreams 109

17   The Button 115

18   The Pit 121

19   Abnormal, Paranormal, Supernormal 129

20   Cats Are Spies 133

21   End of Days 141

22   Man of Genius 149

23   Creepier Karpis 155

24   Midnight 161

25   Farkas Fracas 167

26   Christmas Day 173

    Meet the Cast 179

    After-credits Scene 184

RACE AGAINST TIME

Liam Chapman started every day the same way: in a white-knuckled race against time.

Beep! Beep! Bee—

Slam!

Liam silenced his alarm clock by slamming the snot out of it. Most kids use phones or parents to wake them up, but Liam preferred this clunky digital clock with an out-of-date iPhone dock because it was so slammable. He rolled out of bed and took two steps before opening his eyes.

Sixty seconds.

Liam stumbled down the stairs in a way that suggested his legs hadn't quite woken up at the same time as the top half of his body. Downstairs in the kitchen, he grabbed a banana from the counter and a backpack from the chair.

"Byemomndad," Liam mumbled to his parents.

"Liam!" his mom said. "I'll drive . . ."

Liam couldn't concentrate on the rest of her sentence with the countdown ticking in his head.

Forty-seven seconds.

In exactly forty-seven seconds, Mrs. Kessling would pull the school bus up to the corner of Matilda Street and Dearborne Avenue. Mrs. Kessling was never late—even by one second. Anyone who wasn't standing at the intersection's southwest corner by 7:17 a.m. would get left behind. Mrs. Kessling had a schedule to keep.

Liam had a schedule to keep, too. Sure, he *could* set his alarm a few minutes earlier. That might free enough time to wear something besides school clothes to bed or choose a hairstyle other than "tumbleweed." But that wouldn't be nearly as much fun as seeing the scowl on Mrs. Kessling's face every morning when he jumped onto the bus just in time.

Liam jammed his feet into his shoes without bothering to untie them. He'd perfected the art of wriggling his foot at just the right angle to slip inside rather than crushing the back and turning the shoe into a flip-flop. He flung open the side door, took three steps down the driveway, then made a noise that sounded like a half-croak, half-gasp.

"Ahhgck?"

Dearborne Avenue—a quiet street that ended in an even quieter cul-de-sac—had transformed into an absolute circus. Greasy men with greasy beards crowded the sidewalk. A van painted with the words "CATS ARE SPIES!" had parked in front of his house. Multiple people carried bullhorns.

Thirty-nine seconds.

Liam took a quick breath and started running.

"No cuts!" a man wearing a leather jacket covered in five hundred patches yelled as Liam squeezed past.

"This is my driveway!" Liam yelled back.

"Back of the line!" someone dressed as Bigfoot growled.

"Just trying to get to the bus!"

"No one's getting on my bus!" another voice yelled.

Liam glanced left just in time to notice a rusty bus with an inflatable alien and U.F.O. tied to its roof. The alien held a sign that read, "U.F.UH-OH THE GOVERNMENT IS LYING TO YOU."

Twenty-seven seconds.

Liam considered crossing the street but noticed a police officer watching everyone with wary eyes. Liam couldn't get arrested for jaywalking on his own street! He heard the familiar rumble of the bus and started sprinting faster.

Twenty-one seconds.

Liam hurdled someone camping on the sidewalk . . .

Twenty seconds.

. . . sidestepped a camerawoman . . .

Nineteen seconds.

. . . and crashed into Mortimer Pitts.

Mortimer Pitts hosted the beloved Mocha with Morty in the Morning segment on Channel 5 News. He'd won multiple Regional Daytime Emmy awards for his delightful reporting on local businesses and wacky events. And now, for some reason, he'd planted himself right in Liam's way.

"Oof!" Liam bounced off of the reporter and fell to the ground.

Morty Pitts, ever the professional, flashed his Regional Daytime Emmy–winning smile to the camera and offered a hand to Liam. "Looks like we have one eager shopper. Son, can you tell me . . ."

No, Liam couldn't. He had a bus to catch.

Seven seconds.

Liam mumbled an apology and took off toward the bus. The last kids were walking on now.

Six. Five. Four.

Liam wasn't going to make it. He locked eyes with Mrs. Kessling. Her mouth curled into a smile that looked eerily similar to the Grinch's right before he robs all the Whos.

Three. Two. One.

Mrs. Kessling reached to close the bus door, then squawked when she saw that Elsa Rutledge had stopped to tie her shoe with one foot on the sidewalk and one foot on the bus stair.

"Get on the bus! Get on right now!" Mrs. Kessling commanded.

Elsa fumbled with her laces like she was a five-year-old instead of a fifth-grader.

Liam dodged one final man trying to hand him a cryptozoology pamphlet and slid around Elsa onto the bus.

"Hi, Mrs. Kessling!"

Mrs. Kessling's face settled into a scowl even more disgusted than normal. Liam plopped into a seat, and Elsa sat next to him a second later.

"Thanks," Liam whispered.

Elsa nodded a slight acknowledgment.

As the bus started rolling, Liam looked out the window. The line of weirdos stretched across the intersection all the way down Dearborne Avenue's cul-de-sac. Liam craned his neck to try glimpsing where everyone was headed. Suddenly, it hit him. Liam's eyes widened, and he leaped to his feet.

"STOP THE BUS!"

2 ⚡

THE MAD SCIENTIST
DOWN THE STREET

Mrs. Kessling, of course, did not stop the bus. "SIT DOWN!"

"I need . . ."

Elsa grabbed Liam's shirt and yanked him into the seat.

"But, but, but . . ." Liam gestured wildly toward the big brick house at the end of the cul-de-sac. He desperately wanted to do more than gesture, but he'd only been awake for 90 seconds, and his mouth still needed a bit more time to connect with his brain. Elsa waited patiently for Liam's body to finish booting up. Finally, he calmed down enough to say, "The garage sale's today!"

"Yeah, I see that."

"I need to go!"

"You actually need a mint." Elsa fished in her backpack for the tin of mints she kept for Liam.

"This is a once-in-a-lifetime thing!" Liam said.

"You know what would be a once-in-a-lifetime thing?"

"Like, nobody knows what's inside that house! NOBODY! They should let us off of school for this!"

"You brushing your teeth in the morning. That would be a once-in-a-lifetime thing." Elsa held out a mint.

Liam was absolutely befuddled that Elsa was not taking this more seriously. "You know who lived there, right?!"

"Mmhmm."

"Professor Wolfgang Snellenburg!"

"Right."

"They made a documentary about him!"

"I know. Take the mint."

Most conversations between Liam and Elsa went like this. Although they were so close in age that they recently had a joint birthday party at the skating rink, Elsa acted quite a bit older than Liam. She already had a Red Cross babysitting certification and college savings account, while Liam already had four cavities.

Liam popped the mint into his mouth. "What do you think happened to him? I know a lot of people say that something blew up, but the documentary made it sound like alien stuff."

Elsa shook her head and looked out the window.

"Come on." Liam poked her.

"It happened before I moved here."

"So? You had to have watched the documentary. That's your thing, right? Documentaries? Cuz they're educational?"

"Why do you suddenly care so much?" Elsa asked. "You've never said a single thing about him, and now this garage sale is the most important thing that's ever happened."

Liam shrugged. "A mad scientist lived down the street. Why wouldn't I care? Plus, there's this." Liam pulled a thick book out of his backpack titled, *Man of Genius.*

"Is that about him?" Elsa asked.

"No. Thomas Edison. It's for our oral book report tomorrow. At first, I was gonna do something lame like tie a key to a kite . . ."

"For Thomas Edison?" Elsa interrupted.

"Yeah. Cuz that's how he invented electricity. Anyways, I realized my talk would be way better if I bought some science stuff from the garage sale!"

Elsa looked like she had ten different things to explain to Liam, but finally settled for, "Maybe you should read the book instead."

"Yeah, OK," Liam scoffed as if this was the silliest suggestion he'd ever heard. "But seriously, all the good stuff's gonna be gone when I get back. Now I don't know what to do for my report."

"Read the book?"

"Maybe I can learn a magic trick or something."

Liam spent the rest of the ride pouting. He should have prepared better. Not for the book report, obviously, but for the garage sale. Professor Snellenburg wasn't famous in the same way that movie stars and athletes are, but he was certainly a celebrity among the type of people who own Bigfoot costumes and post wild theories to the internet. Oddballs had been trekking to Dearborne Avenue for years to catch a glimpse of the mysterious professor. Of course, a garage sale at the Snellenburg house would turn into a convention for kooks.

When Liam stepped off the bus, a grating voice snapped him out of his funk. "LAME!"

One time in third grade, Liam's teacher had accidentally called him "Lame" instead of "Liam." It'd happened so fast that most of the class missed it. Know who definitely didn't miss it? Mason Farkas. Mason had single-handedly kept the nickname alive for two full years.

"Mason."

Mason gave Liam a punch in the arm that was just a notch above playful. "You're famous, Lame! You were on TV this morning. I watched it in the Tesla."

Teslas are expensive electric cars so fancy that they have a giant TV screen built right in the middle of the dashboard.

Mr. Farkas drove a Tesla, a fact that Mason somehow found a way to work into every single conversation.

"Morty really flattened you, huh?"

"It didn't hurt that bad."

Mason wrapped his arm around Liam. "Can't believe I know someone famous. Famous Lamous. Maybe that's what I'll call you."

"Not your best work, Mason," Elsa said.

"You're not the best work, Grandma!"

Mason's nickname for Elsa had been "Let It Go" until the day Elsa let it slip that she was named after her grandmother, not *Frozen*. Fair enough. "Grandma" fit her way better anyway.

"Hey, Famous Lamous, I might visit you after school. I'll be on your street."

"Garage sale?" Liam asked.

"Gonna pick up some science junk for my report. I'm doing mine on Nick Tesla. He's the guy who invented Tesla."

"He's not . . ." Elsa cut herself off and groaned at the sky. "Why doesn't anyone just read the book?!"

GARAGE SALE
OF THE CENTURY

After school, Liam ran to the big house at the end of the cul-de-sac. Maybe there was still time to grab a Bunsen burner or lab coat or maybe a . . .

Oh.

It looked like a bomb had gone off. That's both in the figurative sense (the place was a complete mess) and literal (grass in the front yard had been burnt in a black ring). All the folding tables were empty and all the customers had gone home. Well, almost all the customers.

"You missed it, Lame!" Mason walked down the driveway carrying a cardboard box overflowing with crusty, old junk. "The garage sale of the century! Shouldn't have taken the bus."

Mason opened the door to his dad's Tesla and started to set the box on the backseat.

"I don't think so!" Mr. Farkas said.

"But Dad, I . . ."

"That's not going in the Tesla. Mom can pick you up in the Camry." With that, Mr. Farkas drove away.

"Should have taken the bus," Liam said. He walked up the driveway feeling so cool. That was a great quip! Liam never had quips.

Liam stopped before reaching the garage to take a closer look at Professor Snellenburg's house. He'd never been this close before. The brick house was so much bigger and older than any of the other homes on the street that it felt like the neighborhood had been built around it. From Liam's end of Dearborne Avenue, the house and forest behind it always looked like they'd been lifted from a black-and-white monster movie. Up close, however, things felt a little more friendly. It was still no vacation home, but small touches like the gnome in the weed-covered flower bed showed someone had at least tried making the place a little homier at one time.

"Liam! You're not going to say hi?" a cheery voice said.

Liam spun around. Elsa's mom was picking trash off the ground. "Oh!" Liam said. "What are you doing here?!"

"Just trying to help. This place was a mess. Here." She handed Liam the crumpled pamphlet she'd picked up entitled, "Temporal Rifts and You."

Liam glanced around for a trash can. When he didn't see one, he stuffed the pamphlet into his pocket. "Did my mom help too?"

"Um, no," Mrs. Rutledge said. "I'm just . . ."

"Excuse me! Excuse me, ma'am!" an agitated voice called.

Liam turned to see that the CATS ARE SPIES van from earlier that morning was now parked in the driveway. A bushy-eyebrowed man marched toward them. Liam shot a worried glance toward Mrs. Rutledge.

"Hello," the man said before Mrs. Rutledge could greet him. "I bought some blue barrels earlier this morning, and, uh, can you, ummmm . . . well, like, what was in them and what if someone drank it?"

Mrs. Rutledge's eyes widened. "You drank something out of a barrel?!"

"No! But if someone did, and they're now experiencing abdominal discomfort . . ."

Mrs. Rutledge turned to Liam. "I have to take care of this. Let me know if you need anything, OK?"

Liam nodded and wandered into the garage. At this point, he'd settle for a coffee cup if it looked science-y enough. Unfortunately, he couldn't even find that. The best he could do was a crate full of empty baby food jars. Liam picked up one of the jars and held it above his head. Maybe he could trap a lightning bug in here. That felt like something Thomas Edison would do.

As he stared through the jar, Liam spotted a shelf near the ceiling. The shelf held only one thing, and it was covered by a blue tarp. Liam slowly lowered the jar, then stared at the tarp blob for awhile. It looked like a box roughly the size of the one Mason had been carrying. What could it be? The longer Liam stared, the more the mystery box felt like a present wrapped just for him. He turned around. Mrs. Rutledge was still talking to the cat guy. Mason was staring at his phone. No one else was around.

This was Liam's one chance to walk away from the garage sale with something cool. He dragged a folding table over to the shelf and climbed on top of it. Close. He emptied the baby food jars out of the crate, then stacked the crate upside-down on top of the table. Almost. Finally, he arranged a few of the jars on top of the crate into a step stool just wide enough to stand on. That did the trick.

Liam climbed his wobbly tower and tugged on the tarp. Nine times out of ten, that tug would unleash an avalanche of junk on Liam's head. But not today. Today was a day of destiny. Today, the tug was just strong enough to coax the cardboard box off of the shelf and into Liam's waiting arms. Liam caught the box and gingerly stepped off of his rickety death tower.

Back on the ground, he peeked into the box. There was an old rotary dial telephone. A lantern half-filled with orange goo. Typewriter keys. The guts of a speaker. A tangle of wires, cables, string, and plugs. And it all smelled like wet basement.

Liam couldn't have imagined anything better.

Liam felt bad about taking the off-limits box, but he told himself that anything inside the garage is fair game during a garage sale. He fished in his pocket and pulled out all the money he'd brought: three dollars. Liam took a deep breath and approached Mrs. Rutledge, who was still talking to the cat guy.

"If you just let me call poison control . . ." Mrs. Rutledge reasoned.

"But we don't *know* it's poison!" Cat Guy fired back.

Liam waved. "Mrs. Rutledge, I know you don't work here, but I only have three dollars, and I . . ."

"Wait, you don't even work here?!" Cat Guy said.

Mrs. Rutledge spread her arms. "I'm working! I'm here!"

Cat Guy shook his head. "I want to speak to the manager."

"THIS IS A GARAGE SALE!" Mrs. Rutledge huffed, then turned to Liam and pointed to a cashbox. "You're fine. Just set the money over there."

"Now you're giving discounts?!" Cat Guy sputtered.

Liam paid for his box of junk and hurried down the driveway. He couldn't wait to see the look on Elsa's face when she—

"OOF!"

Liam tripped over Mason's foot, spilling the contents of his box all over the driveway.

"Famous Lamous! That's twice in one day! You've got to be more careful." Mason started picking through Liam's stuff. "Let's see what we've got here . . ."

Liam didn't hear another word Mason said. He'd just seen the words written on the side of his box.

No way was this real.

No.

Way.

Liam blinked. He blinked again.

Four words. Four life-changing words neatly printed in black marker:

WORLD'S WORST TIME MACHINE

4

BYOC

Time machine.

Time. Machine.

TIME MACHINE! A MACHINE THAT CONTROLS TIME!

"Ooh, a broken antenna! What are you gonna do with this, Lame?"

Mason's voice snapped Liam back to reality. Mason hadn't seen the words, right? Liam quickly scooped everything into the box. The time machine box. *His* time machine box. He had to get it home. *Now.* "Good luck on your, uh, your thing," Liam mumbled as he hurried off.

"Good luck on not tripping!" Mason called back.

Liam sprinted so fast that he nearly did trip four times. Finally, he ran up his driveway and burst into the house. His mom, who was working at the kitchen table, gave him a weird look from behind her laptop. "You OK?"

"I (*gasp*) got (*gasp*) a (*gasp, gasp, gasp*) . . ." Liam bent over and wheezed. Finally, he caught his breath enough to finish the most important two words of the sentence. "Time machine."

"A what?" his mom asked.

Liam set the box down and turned it around so his mom could read the writing.

Mom squinted, then smirked. "The worst time machine, huh?"

"Well—well, yeah, but it's still a time machine."

"Let's see it!"

Liam clunked the box on the ground next to the kitchen table and beamed. He decided right then and there that his mom would be the first person to get a ride in the time machine. Liam would take her anywhere she wanted. She was always buying old farmhouse stuff for decorations—maybe she'd want to go back in time to meet some real prairie farm people.

Mom narrated her dig through the box. "Wowww . . . Haven't seen one of these for a long time . . . Gonna need to duct tape that . . . Why is everything so sticky?" When she reached the bottom of the box, she looked up at Liam. "Where's the clock?"

"Huh?"

"It's a time machine. It needs a clock, right?"

"I—I haven't looked at the instructions yet."

"Or is this one of those BYOC time machines?"

"I don't know what that means."

Mom grinned. "Bring your own clock."

Liam's face fell. His mom thought this was a joke, didn't she? It hadn't even occurred to Liam that someone might not believe in the time machine. "It's real!"

"Oh, of course, of course!"

"It's from Professor Snellenburg's house!"

"I think that's amazing." Liam's mom continued smiling, but it was clearly a "this is cute" smile rather than a "this is the most amazing thing that has ever happened" smile.

"You know what?" Liam picked up the box and turned toward the stairs. "You'll see."

"Oh! Hon. No greasy boxes upstairs. Um, you can take it downstairs to the scary side if you want."

Liam huffed and carried the box to the basement. The Chapman basement was split into two sections that the family still referred to by the nicknames Liam had given them when he was three years old: the comfy-cozy side and the scary side. The comfy-cozy side of the basement had thick carpet, the old living room couch, a TV for video games, and a big sign that read, "Home is where the love is." The scary side had no such welcoming sign. It was unfinished with cement floors, bare light bulbs, Dad's workbench, and years of junk shoved against the wall in half-organized piles. Liam cleared off a spot on his dad's workbench and dumped the box.

Now, where to begin? Oh! There! Someone had typed the words "Model A-537 Manual" on a sheet of paper and stapled it to a bunch more sheets of paper. Liam opened the manual and flipped through it. There was page after page of typed instructions to go along with hand-drawn illustrations.

STEP 1: Secure a corrugated cardboard box. The box should be sturdy, but not too thick. Double-wall construction is best, but in the event of . . .

Blah, blah, blah.

Cardboard box. Great, Liam had one. He flipped it upside-down like the illustration showed and moved on to step number two.

This was going to be fun.

WORLD'S WORST TIME MACHINE

Liam did his best to follow the manual. Actually, that's not true. Doing his best would probably have involved reading the manual. Unfortunately, the manual was full of long words written in an old typewriter font that made them look extra boring, so Liam mostly followed the pictures.

By 7:09 p.m., the project was complete. Liam stepped back to admire his handiwork. Tubes and wires stuck out of the box at odd angles. The telephone was wired to a portable CD player, which hooked into the guts of an inkjet printer. The entire machine was held together with duct tape and those twist ties that come with loaves of bread.

It was perfect.

Sure, there were a few extra parts. Sure, the power cable plugged directly into cardboard. And, sure, the final step stressed the importance of an all-important "little button" when there definitely was no button. But this was going to work. Liam felt sure of it.

"Mom!" he called upstairs. "It's ready!"

No response.

"Dad!"

Liam heard the sound of audience laughter coming from the living room. Oh, right. It was *Wheel of Fortune* time. Even though they had a million things to watch on TV, Liam's parents still found time for *Wheel of Fortune* and *Jeopardy!* every night at 7 p.m.

Liam started walking up the stairs, then had a better idea. He grabbed his tablet from the basement couch, started a video chat, then tapped Elsa's face. After a few seconds, she appeared on the screen.

"Elsaaa!" Liam said in that exaggerated tone people only use when they're on camera. "Guess what I bought at the garage sale?!"

"A light bulb?"

"Way better!"

"Because Thomas Edison invented the light bulb. I feel like you should at least know that for your report."

"Look!" Liam flipped the camera so Elsa could see the time machine. "Now, it doesn't look like much, but . . ."

"Where did you get that?" Elsa interrupted.

"Garage sale. I already told you."

"Liam. Do not touch that."

"It's a time machine!" Liam held up the power cord. "You're going to be the first to see it in action."

"No! You have to . . ."

Liam plugged the machine into the wall. As soon as he did that, Elsa's face disappeared from the screen, and her voice started breaking up.

"Don't . . ."

". . . Parents . . ."

". . . Over . . ."

". . . Now."

CONNECTION LOST.

Liam tried calling Elsa back, but the app said she was unavailable. He turned his attention back to the time machine. The manual had given lots of instructions for assembling the machine but remained curiously silent about how to actually travel back in time. Liam looked for this elusive "button" from the instructions. Maybe it was on the machine's phone. He picked up the telephone receiver.

Hmmmmmmmmm.

Liam gasped. The phone was making the droning sound that his grandma's would make while it waited for you to dial a number. This was really working! Liam had no idea how to dial these old phones, so he tried spinning the plastic circle in the middle. He started with a little spin.

Click.

He let go, and the dial wound back into place.

Hmmmmmmmmm.

Same noise. What if he tried a big spin?

Click. Hmmmmmmmmm.

What a silly way to choose numbers. He spun again.

Click. Hmmmmmmmmm.

Liam tried the dial once more, and something remarkable happened.

Click.

The droning stopped. In its place was a faint swishing sound.

"He—hello?" Liam said.

No answer.

"Um, I'd like to travel back in time?"

Nothing.

So maybe this wasn't a normal time machine. Mom was right—it didn't even have a clock. What if, instead of traveling back in time, it let you talk to someone from history? Liam could only think of one historical figure at the moment.

"Thomas Edison, please?" Liam croaked.

KKKSHHHHHHHH!

The phone blasted static.

"AH!" Liam slammed the receiver and rubbed his ear.

Blurp.

The box made a sound very much like a belch. A wisp of black smoke drifted out of it. Liam squinted and crept closer to the box.

BUUURRRRRP!

This sound was accompanied by a much larger cloud of black smoke blown right in Liam's face.

"Ahhhhhh!"

The smoke burned his eyes . . .

Cough, choke, wheeeeeeze!

. . . Got in his lungs . . .

Gaaaaaaaaag!

. . . And filled his mouth with the taste of gasoline mixed with taco meat.

Thunk-thunk-thunk-thunk.

Unfortunately, the smoke burp was just the time machine's opening act. The box started rumbling. Then, it began bouncing.

THUNK-THUNK-THUNK-THUNK!

Liam tried pulling the power cord out of the wall. It wouldn't budge. Also, that just seemed to make the machine angrier. The box lunged like a snarling dog on a leash.

Ka-CHUNK! Ka-CHUNK! Ka-CHUNK!

Liam fell down, screamed, and scooted away from the time machine. Finally, it ran out of steam.

PUUUUUUUuuuuuuuutz.

With that, it spit out one final cloud of taco-gas smoke.

Liam had the good sense to keep his mouth, nose, and eyes closed this time. But someone else didn't.

Cough!

"Hello?" Liam called.

A figure stood up in the smoke. Then, it bent over in a coughing fit.

Cough! Hack! Crooaaak!

Could this really be Thomas Edison? The figure was shorter than Liam expected. Skinnier, too.

"Who is it?" Liam asked.

Eventually, the figure emerged from the smoke. It was a . . . boy. A boy with wild hair and red suspenders and pants that were too short to be pants, but too long to be shorts. He also held a small bronze Scottie dog statue for some reason. The boy squinted at Liam.

"Are you . . . Thomas Edison?" Liam whispered.

The boy didn't answer. Instead, he growled, cocked the Scottie dog behind his head, and charged at Liam.

TOMMY TWINKLES

"Wait!"

That was all Liam got out before the kid hit him square in the chest. He drove Liam back into a pile of Christmas decorations.

"Oof!"

A wreath fell over the kid's head as both boys hit the ground hard.

"Hey!" Liam's dad called from upstairs. "Everything OK down there?"

Liam locked eyes with the boy who still held the Scottie dog statue like he intended to use it as a weapon. "Uh, yeah!" Liam yelled back. "Sorry!" Then, he slowly whispered, "You're Thomas Edison, right? My name's Liam. Liam Chapman."

"What is this?" The boy's eyes darted all around.

"This is the future," Liam whispered. "You're in my basement. I'm doing a book report on you tomorrow."

The boy blinked. His whole expression changed.

"You're doing a book report? On me?"

Liam nodded. He found it a little strange that this was the sentence Thomas Edison had chosen to focus on rather than the "future" part.

". . . If you're doing a report on me, then I must be famous," Thomas Edison said almost to himself.

"Well, yeah," Liam said. "You're Thomas Edison."

"Hot dog, I'm famous!" Thomas Edison ripped the wreath off his neck and threw it like a Frisbee. He grabbed Liam's shoulders and started jumping. "I'M FAMOUS!"

Liam jumped too. "You're one of the most famous people ever!"

"I knew I was going to make it! 'Remember the name,' I told those crumbs! They laughed at me. WHO'S LAUGHING NOW?!"

"Haha!" Liam laughed.

"Tell me everything I do!" Thomas Edison said.

Liam stopped jumping. "OK, well, you need to understand that I didn't read the whole book. But, did you do the kite thing yet?"

"What kite thing?"

"You know, where you fly the kite during a thunderstorm? Like, you tie a key on the string or something?"

Now, it was Edison's turn to stop jumping. "That's Benjamin Franklin."

"Oh! Right. Well, you definitely invent the light bulb."

"No, no, no, no!" Edison looked like he wanted to cry.

"It's OK! Light bulbs are good. Really good!"

"I know they are."

"Wait, how do you know if you haven't invented them yet?"

"Because I'm not *that* Thomas Edison!"

Liam didn't know what to say. "Um, are you sure?"

Thomas Edison gritted his teeth. "I HATE that Thomas Edison." He balled up his fists. "Don't ever say that name around me again."

Liam held up his hands. "Just tell me what to call you!"

"Tommy Twinkles. You've heard of Tommy Twinkles, haven't you?"

Liam had definitely never heard of Tommy Twinkles, but he wasn't about to say that to someone who'd just tackled him. "Sounds familiar."

Tommy relaxed. "Soon, everyone will know the name."

Liam nodded, eager to call this kid whatever he wanted as long as it kept him calm. "They sure will, Tommy."

"And you're going to tell the world about me, right?"

"Um, uh, well . . ."

"With your report!"

"Of course! Yeah, yeah, yeah."

"Then start writing!"

Liam scrambled to find paper and a pencil. "Right! OK, so, um, what year are you from?"

"1933."

"Cool! Good year."

"No, it's not."

"Ohhhkay, and what should I say about you?"

"That I'm the greatest gangster who's ever lived."

Liam looked over the skinny kid who couldn't be older than ten, but by now, he knew not to argue. "Got it. Greatest gangster. Check. My class will be very impressed. Glad we got you Tommy Tinkles."

"Twinkles!"

"Tommy Twinkles, sorry."

"Ever heard of Al Capone?" Tommy asked.

"Sure."

"John Dillinger?"

"Absolutely." Liam wrote down "John Dillybar" as a reminder to look up this apparently famous person.

"Amateurs." Tommy said.

"Yeah. Right. I was thinking that too. So you rob banks and stuff?"

"Better." Tommy slammed the bronze Scottie dog onto Mr. Chapman's workbench. "Sleepy Barkis."

Liam nodded and scribbled that down. His notebook now contained the words, "Tommy Twinkles," "John Dillybar," and "Sleepy Barkis," which would not be very helpful clues for the police if he were to disappear right now.

"Sleepy Barkis belongs to Creepy Karpis, the scariest gangster in the world," Tommy explained. "Karpis has a soft spot for the old mutt, so he got a statue made." He held up the figurine. "I just stole that statue."

"Why?!" Liam asked.

"I told you! Because I'm the greatest gangster of all time!" Suddenly, Tommy's eyes lit up, and he started marching toward the stairs. "Shake a leg."

"Wait! Where are we going?"

"To rob a bank." Tommy said. "A bank of the future."

Ding-dong!

Just then, Liam's doorbell rang.

7

CHEETOS

"The coppers!" Tommy shrieked.

Was it really the police? Officers had never shown up at Liam's door before, but then again, neither had an amateur gangster. Maybe it was the time police.

Tommy scrambled under the workbench. "Holler when the coast is clear."

Ding-dong.

Liam ran upstairs, but his mom beat him to the front door. "Elsa! Hi! Is that for Liam's time machine?"

Liam peeked around the corner to see Elsa holding one of those old alarm clocks with bells on top. She quickly covered it and flashed an extra-big smile at Mom. "Oh! You know about the time machine?" Elsa was trying to play it cool, but her red cheeks and tangled hair made it clear that she'd sprinted over.

Mrs. Chapman smiled like this was the most adorable thing she'd ever seen. "I told him he needed a clock, but he never listens to me. Can I get you two scientists a snack?"

"Mom . . ." Liam said.

"OK, OK, I'll stop." Mrs. Chapman misinterpreted the look of terror on her son's face for embarrassment. "Just let me know if you need anything."

"No, there's something . . ."

"What's that?" a voice asked from the kitchen. Everyone turned to see Tommy staring at the living room TV.

Liam's mom looked at Tommy, then at the TV. "It's, uh, it's *Wheel of Fortune*." She glanced back at Tommy. Specifically, his suspenders. "I'm sorry, are you in Liam's class?"

Tommy shook his head. "Name's Tommy. Tommy Twinkles."

Liam's mom opened her mouth to ask a question, but she had so many questions at the same time that none came out.

Elsa filled the silence with a big, fake laugh. "Classic Tommy! Anyways, I'll take that snack, Mrs. Chapman. Do you have Cheetos?"

Liam's mom shook her head. "Pretzels."

"OK, never mind!" Elsa stepped past a stunned Mrs. Chapman and herded Liam and Tommy toward the basement. "Don't worry about us! We'll see you in a bit!"

"I'm watching the wheel," Tommy complained when Elsa tried pushing him toward the basement. She pinched his arm. "Jeepers!" he squealed.

Down in the basement, Elsa glanced at her alarm clock, nodded, then pushed it into Liam's chest. "Hold this." She turned her attention to the time machine.

"Hey, toots." Tommy winked at Elsa.

"Don't call me 'toots,'" Elsa started rearranging wires. "And don't move. I'm sending you back home."

"I'm not going back." Tommy stuffed the bronze dog into his pocket and turned toward the stairs.

"Get him," Elsa commanded Liam.

"Um," Liam fumbled. "So we want to be careful about . . ."

"Get him!"

"Argh!" Tommy spun and acted like he was going to charge at Liam again, which caused Liam to stumble back and fall. Tommy chuckled at that, then wiggled his fingers when he spotted a Dubble Bubble bucket across the room. "Ooh!"

"This would be so much easier with Cheetos," Elsa muttered as she turned back to the time machine.

Liam's head was spinning. "Do you know what's going on here?" he asked Elsa.

"Obviously."

"OK, cuz I have no idea."

"Obviously."

Elsa didn't offer any further information, which was maddening to Liam. "So, so, so you need to tell me!" Liam's voice squeaked at the end of that sentence.

"No, you need to start listening to me."

"I've been listening to you this whole time!"

"Oh, really?" Elsa spun around. "Because I told you to read the book. You clearly didn't read the book, or you wouldn't have had time to build this. Then, I told you not to tell your parents."

"The video was kind of cutting out there, so I never heard you say that."

"You told your parents anyways. Then—and this is a big one—I told you not to touch it. Video wasn't cutting out there, was it?"

Liam shrugged.

"So you not only touched the machine, but you *plugged it in*, and now here we are with—" Elsa waved her hand toward Tommy. "Timmy or whatever his name is."

"Thomas Edison," Liam said.

"Tommy Twinkles," Tommy corrected.

"Great," Elsa said. "So please listen closely when I tell you to keep Mr. Twinkles busy while I fix everything you broke."

"This ain't gum!" Tommy yelled when he finally got the Dubble Bubble bucket open, only to discover that it was full of random screws.

"Good news!" Liam's mom announced from the top of the stairs. "I found Cheetos!"

Elsa froze.

"Now, let's see this big project you're working on."

"NO!" Elsa shouted. "Turn around!"

Liam shot Elsa a weird look. She'd never talked to an adult like that before. But one glance at her face revealed that she wasn't trying to be bossy or disrespectful. Something had her absolutely terrified.

Mrs. Chapman did not turn around. Instead, she walked all the way down the stairs and turned toward the scary side of the basement so she could see the time machine. "Ohhhhhhh!" she said in that tone parents use when admiring their three-year-old's artwork. "It's so . . ."

Blurp.

A wisp of black smoke curled out of the machine. Mrs. Chapman turned to her son with wide eyes. "Did . . . Did that thing just burp?"

"Please, please, please leave!" Elsa pleaded.

BUUURRRRRP!

The time machine spat a cloud of black smoke, then started chugging and bouncing.

"Go, go, go!" Elsa tried pushing Mom back upstairs. She reached the second stair before the time machine pulled off its final trick.

ZAAAAAAP!

A purple bolt shot out of the machine, snaked around Elsa, and zapped Mom. She disappeared instantly, dropping the bag of Cheetos to the ground. The whole thing happened so fast that Liam could only stand in shock for several seconds. Once reality caught up to him, he started screaming.

"MOOOOOM!"

"What's wrong?!" Dad yelled from upstairs.

"Nonononono!" the kids warned.

Footsteps thumped across the kitchen. Liam ran to the time machine and tried yanking the plug from the wall. Still stuck.

THUD-THUD-THUD-THUD

Liam's dad barreled down the stairs two at a time and skidded to a stop in front of the time machine. He turned to Liam. "Where's Mom?"

ZAAAAAAP!

Liam's dad disappeared, too.

8

CHAOS

"I don't know why I even bother to talk," Elsa said.

"MOM!" Liam screamed.

Crunch, crunch, crunch. Tommy munched Cheetos.

"You do the opposite of what I say. Your parents do the opposite of what I say."

"DAD!" Liam shook the time machine.

Crunch, crunch, crunch.

"Maybe I should start saying the opposite of what I want. Maybe then, people will actually listen to me."

Liam shook Elsa. "WHAT HAPPENED TO THEM?!"

Elsa took a deep breath. "Look. I know this seems bad."

"VERY BAD!"

"But it's not. It happens all the time."

"Wh—wha—what does that mean?!"

"Most adults can't be in the same room as the machine or they'll get sucked in."

"What? WHY?!"

Elsa threw up her hands in frustration. "Because it's a bad time machine! The worst time machine! It says so right on the box."

"But, like, where did they go?!"

"I don't know. Time jail, maybe?" When Elsa saw the terror on Liam's face, she changed her answer. "Actually, why don't we call it a waiting room? A nice, comfortable waiting room."

"So we can get them back?"

"Oh yeah. Well—" Elsa glanced around the basement. "Where's the meter?"

"The what?"

Elsa stepped over Tommy, who was sitting on the floor eating Cheetos by the fistful. She finally found the alarm clock lying on the ground behind him. She picked it up, tapped its face, then held it to her ear. "You can't drop this. It's very sensitive."

"Elsa," Liam tried again. "We can get them back, right?"

"Yes, we can get them back. Look." She turned the clock around.

Liam hadn't noticed before, but the clock was divided into three sections. Twelve to four o'clock was green, Four to eight o'clock was yellow, and eight to twelve o'clock was red. The clock hands had been replaced by a single needle, and right now, that needle was pointing at one.

"This is a chaos meter," Elsa explained. "Whenever you change history, you cause chaos. A little chaos is fine, but too much chaos causes bad stuff to happen."

"What kind of stuff?"

Elsa sighed. "I'd tell you if I could. I really would. But nothing causes chaos faster than talking. I can control what I say, but I can't control what you say."

"I won't say anything," Liam said.

"Oh, I know you won't." Elsa turned to examine the time machine. "Once I rewind time, Tommy goes home, your parents come back, and nobody remembers this ever happened."

"Nobody remembers?!"

"I'm sorry, *you* won't remember, but I will," Elsa said with a wink. "And don't worry, I'll make sure you never see this machine again." She then started removing wires.

Liam was reeling. As an only child, he'd dreamed about having a sibling his whole life. Then, just over a year ago, Elsa's family moved to the neighborhood. In that short time, the Chapmans and Rutledges had become family. The moms went running every morning. Liam knew how to make Elsa's baby brother Ollie laugh like no one else. Elsa borrowed Liam's roller blades so often that they might as well be hers. At times, Liam felt like Elsa was his actual sister, and now he was learning that she was—what, some sort of time traveler?

"Are you from the future?" Liam whispered.

"No," Elsa replied without looking up from her work.

"But this is your time machine, right?"

"No."

"Then, how do you know about it?"

Elsa shook her head and tapped the chaos meter. Then, she stepped back, folded her arms, and furrowed her brow. "Where's the recombobulator?"

"The what?"

Elsa got down on her hands and knees to look under the workbench. "The recombobulator. You discombobulated time, now we have to recombobulate it. It's the thing that looks like a lantern. Has orange goo inside."

"Oh! It was in the box."

"Well, it's not here now. Where did you put it?"

Liam thought for a moment. The lantern was one of the first things he'd noticed at the garage sale, but he didn't remember seeing it while assembling the time machine. "Tommy, have you seen a lantern?" he asked.

Tommy was still munching Cheetos on the floor with a faraway look in his eyes.

"Tommy." Liam snapped his fingers. "Hey, Tommy!" Tommy didn't look up. Liam shot Elsa a worried glance.

Elsa sighed. "If you want to calm someone from the past, you give them Cheetos. It's more flavor than they've ever experienced. Their brains can't handle it, so they just kind of zone out. We have to wait for him to finish now."

"I don't think the lantern's here," Liam said. "I ran home pretty fast after the garage sale. Maybe it fell out. Is it important?"

Elsa closed her eyes. "It's the only way to erase chaos. I can't rewind time if I can't erase the chaos."

"Then let's go!" Liam turned toward the stairs.

"Wait." Elsa dug through the extra time machine parts on the workbench until she pulled out a headlamp. Liam had stayed away from the lamp earlier because its elastic band looked and smelled like it'd been retrieved from a dumpster. "Put this on."

Liam wrinkled his nose and strapped the lamp to his head. Elsa then unplugged the time machine's telephone receiver from its cord and plugged the cord into a port on the headlamp.

"OK," Elsa said as she fiddled with a dial on the time machine. "Stare straight ahead and focus on the moment you left the garage sale."

"Is this gonna zap my brain?" Liam asked.

"Not if you hold still."

Liam held very, very still, while Elsa flipped a switch on the time machine. After a few seconds, the headlamp started projecting a fuzzy image onto the wall. Liam gasped. Then, he shrieked and rubbed his head.

"I told you to hold still," Elsa said. "Try again."

Liam took a deep breath before returning to the memory. The image flickered back on, then sharpened. There, playing on the wall, was a video of Liam walking down Professor Snellenburg's driveway. Only, the scene wasn't from Liam's point of view. It was an overhead view like from a security camera. "How's it doing that?" Liam whispered.

"Concentrate."

Liam watched himself pay Mrs. Rutledge and walk down the driveway. He found that the harder he concentrated, the closer the camera zoomed into the scene. He finally zoomed close enough to see the lantern sticking out of the box. "The Booboolater!" he yelled.

"Recombobulator," Elsa corrected.

The kids watched Mason trip Liam, sending the recombobulator flying out of the box. Then, they watched Mason shove the device into his own box while Liam gaped at the "World's Worst Time Machine" label.

"He stole it!" Liam yelped.

Elsa sighed and pulled the lamp off of Liam's head. "Let's get it back."

When they turned around, they both froze. An empty bag of Cheetos lay on the ground. Tommy was nowhere to be found. "Tommy?" Liam ran upstairs. "Tommy! TOMMY!"

Elsa joined him in the living room. "Where did he go?!"

"I don't . . ." Suddenly, Liam got a sinking feeling in the pit of his stomach. He knew exactly where Tommy was going. And it was going to cause maximum chaos.

"He's going to rob a bank," Liam whispered. "A bank of the future."

THOMAS EDISON ROBS A BANK

"What is wrong with him?!" Elsa asked as they ran outside.

"He thinks he's a gangster," Liam looked down the street in both directions. No Tommy.

"But he's Thomas Edison!"

"Not that Thomas Edison. Grab your bike."

Elsa ran back home to grab her bicycle, while Liam pulled his out of the garage. Elsa returned a few minutes later with her bike, a backpack, and the chaos meter hanging from her neck on one of her mom's long necklaces. Liam did a double take when he saw the chain, but didn't comment because maybe this was some weird time travel thing he didn't know about.

Elsa noticed the look. "I was gonna stuff it in the backpack, but I figured we need to see it," she explained.

Liam looked closer. The needle was still near the one, but it was wiggling. He took a deep, nervous breath. "Let's go."

The kids raced through the neighborhood. Since Tommy was on foot, Liam figured they'd catch him quickly. No such luck. Twenty minutes later, he pulled over, huffing and puffing. He pointed to the woods at the south end of their neighborhood. "Think he's hiding in there?"

Ding!

Just then, the chaos meter hanging from Elsa's neck dinged. Liam's heart sank when he saw that the needle now pointed at two.

"Wherever he is, he's not hiding," Elsa explained. "People are seeing him. Otherwise, this wouldn't be moving."

Liam spoke faster. "OK, but, but, but there's still lots of room before it hits red, right? So why don't we get that part from Mason now? He lives close. Then, we put it in before Tommy has a chance to do something dumb."

Elsa shook her head. "Tommy is absolutely going to do something dumb. Plus we can't wait 'til the meter hits red. The recombobulator only has enough time slime to work while the meter is green."

Liam got more panicky. "What do you mean 'time slime'?!"

"It's that orange goo in the lantern. You can only heal as much chaos as you have time slime."

More panic now. "You gotta tell me stuff, OK?!" Liam said. "Like, 'hey, this time slime stuff's pretty important,' or 'hey, the machine can zap your parents,' or . . ."

"Hey!" Elsa interrupted Liam to snap him out of his spiral. "Do you trust me?" Liam didn't answer, so Elsa tried again. "I know how you feel, OK? And I know what to do. Trust me, I'm not going to let anything happen to your parents."

Liam slowly nodded.

"Why don't I lead for a little bit?" Elsa asked. She led the way to Prospect Street to check her parents' bank. No sign of Tommy. The kids turned onto Albion Road and tried another bank. Nothing there either. The sun was starting to set. Suddenly—

SCREECH!

Elsa slammed her brakes so hard that Liam had to swerve to avoid running into her. "Look!" she pointed to her left.

"What? Liam asked. "The library?"

"The spaceship library," Elsa replied.

Back in the 1980s, the Fairview County Public Library system decided that the traditional rules of architecture no longer applied to them. So they built a library branch in the shape of a triangle for no reason at all. That felt so good that they built a library with too many staircases. The branch that Elsa and Liam were looking at now—the East Bank branch— had earned the nickname "spaceship library" because it was a perfect circle that looked exactly like a flying saucer.

Liam's eyes widened when he looked at the sign. The East *Bank* branch. "A bank of the future!"

He sped past Elsa up the library driveway. When he rounded the corner, he saw two legs sticking out of the book return chute. "Tommy!"

Just then, a librarian walked out with a key in his hands. "We're closed," he told Liam. Then, he gasped when he saw Tommy's legs. "You can't do that!"

"I'm sorry," Liam said as he tried pulling Tommy out. "He's with me . . ."

"I'm not with this crumb!" Tommy shouted as soon as his head popped free of the book return.

The librarian's face turned red. "Where are your parents?"

"We were just leaving!" Liam wrapped Tommy in his arms and started tugging him backward.

Tommy flung Liam off of him. He was surprisingly strong for how little he weighed. The wannabe gangster then held his finger high in the air. "This is a stickup!"

The librarian clenched his jaw, pulled out his phone, and started dialing.

DING!

The chaos meter announced Elsa's presence as she rounded the corner. "Mr. Kevin!" she called.

The librarian lowered his phone when he saw who was calling his name. "Elsa?"

"I'm so sorry, Mr. Kevin. They're with me."

"Gimme all the money in the till," Tommy growled.

"Hey!" Elsa snapped in front of Tommy's face. "This is a library, OK? That's Mr. Kevin. He's the best librarian here."

Tommy glared at Elsa, then back at Mr. Kevin.

"Now, you apologize," Elsa continued.

Tommy shook his head and skulked off.

"It's getting dark," Mr. Kevin said. "Do you need to use my phone to call your mom?"

Elsa shook her head. "I'll get them home right away."

Mr. Kevin squinted. "Is that an alarm clock around your neck?"

Elsa flashed the fake smile she'd used on Liam's mom. "See you next Tuesday, Mr. Kevin!" She and Liam started pedaling toward Tommy. "And that's why it pays to go to the library," she muttered.

When the kids caught up to Tommy, Elsa motioned for him to hop on the back of Liam's bike. "Gotta go, big guy."

Tommy scoffed. "I'm robbing a bank." He kept walking.

Liam and Elsa exchanged a worried look. They hadn't considered what they might do if Tommy refused to come with them.

"Wait!" Liam said.

Tommy did not wait. Liam caught up with him and asked, "Why do you want to rob a bank so bad?"

"Scram," Tommy said.

"I know you want to be a gangster, but why? Do you need the money? I can give you money."

"I don't want money. I want respect." Tommy spat out the word "respect" like he was quoting a movie line.

"Respect? OK, um, well, I respect you." That didn't earn a response from Tommy, so Liam kept going. "Here's the thing. Gangsters aren't respectable. They go to jail."

Tommy kept walking.

"You know what's respectable?" Liam continued. "A job. A nice, safe desk job. Like an accountant. Why don't you come with us and become an accountant?"

That pitch, to no one's surprise, did not work.

Elsa tried a new tactic. "You like bubble gum, right?"

Tommy slowed.

"Bubble gum has come a looooong way since your time."

"How do you mean?" Tommy asked.

"Come with us, and we'll show you."

Tommy's eyes darted from Elsa to Liam. "Then we'll rob a bank?"

Liam did his best to look confident. "All the banks you can handle."

10

PLAN D

Liam, Elsa, and Tommy gathered at Mason's front door. Liam draped his arm around Tommy's neck in a way that was meant to look friendly, but definitely served as a headlock, while Elsa stuffed the chaos meter into her backpack to avoid another nickname. She took a quick breath, silently rehearsed the plan, then rang the doorbell.

Ding-dong.

A teenage girl answered the door and looked downright disgusted with the sight in front of her. "Mason, your little friends are here!"

A few seconds later, Mason showed up. He looked even more disgusted than his sister. "They're not my friends!" he yelled back into the house before turning to the group. "Grandma. Famous Lamous." He looked over Tommy. "Who's the clown?"

"Mmmnngg," Tommy replied. On the way to Mason's house, Elsa had bought him bubble gum tape from the convenience store and dared him to stuff all six feet into his mouth at once. Challenge accepted. With his mouth full of bubble gum, Tommy couldn't say anything that would ruin the plan.

"That's Tommy," Elsa said. "He's never seen a Tesla before. Could we show him yours?"

Mason sneered. "Yeah, I don't think so." He started closing the door.

OK, that didn't work. Liam stuck his arm in the doorway and initiated Plan B. "Please," he said. "I, um, I . . ." He lowered his voice. "At the garage sale this afternoon, I kinda lost my balance near the Tesla, and, well, I may have scratched it."

Mason's eyes lit up. Good. He was buying the story.

"I mean, I don't know if I scratched it!" Liam continued. "But can I look? Before your dad notices?"

"Really struggling with those noodle legs today, huh, Lame?"

"Hhmmf!" That earned a muffled chuckle from Tommy.

Mason nodded at Tommy and smirked. "I'll open the garage."

While Liam and Elsa both had small garages behind their houses, Mason lived in a mini mansion complete with a fancy three-car attached garage. Mason opened the third door, revealing a shiny silver Tesla hooked up to its charging station. Liam's breath caught when he glimpsed the shelf next to the charging station. There was Mason's box of junk from Professor Snellenburg's garage sale!

"Uh, so, Tommy, this is how you charge a Tesla!" Liam said, covertly pointing Elsa toward the box with a sweep of his arm. "It uses electricity instead of gasoline. How far can it go on a single charge, Mason?"

"Quit stalling, Lame. Where's the scratch?"

Elsa wandered toward the box. Liam needed to stretch this out as long as possible to give her time to check it out. "Anyways, Tommy, I think it goes like eighty miles on a full charge. Isn't that crazy?"

"Three hundred thirty miles!" Mason burst. He couldn't let that gross underestimate slide. "It goes three hundred thirty miles on a single charge. Now where's the scratch?"

Liam made a big show of checking out the rear bumper.

"See it?" Mason asked.

"Not yet." Liam got down on his hands and knees to look under the car. Elsa did the same thing and shook her head. No sighting yet. Now, it was time to trick Mason into leaving them alone for a few minutes. Time for Plan C.

"Ohhhhh," Liam said. "You know what? Now that I think about it, I was probably at the front of the car, not the back."

"Your brain's lame too?" Mason asked. "Lamebrain?"

"Hhmmf!" Another chuckle from Tommy.

Liam circled around to the front of the car with Mason, and sure enough, there was a long scratch across the bumper. "Nooooo!" Liam tried to sell the despair by putting both hands on his face like the screaming emoji. "We have to fix this before your dad sees!"

Mason wrapped his arm around Liam's shoulder. "Hate to see it, Lame. You really hate to see it."

This was going even better than Liam had expected. He was a pretty terrible actor, but Mason wanted him to fail so much that he'd buy anything. Liam turned to Mason with wild eyes. "My dad fixed a scratch on his car with toothpaste before! Could you bring out some toothpaste?"

Mason smirked. "Be right back." He was so excited about Liam's downfall that he nearly skipped into the house.

As soon as Mason disappeared, Liam nudged Tommy and pointed at the scratch. "You can eat the frosting now."

Even though Tommy's mouth was completely full of gum, he managed to stick out his tongue far enough to lick the cake frosting "scratch" right off the car.

Liam gave Elsa a fist bump. "You were so fast!"

"This one's all you," Elsa said. "Frosting was the perfect choice."

"I told you, I saw it in a prank video!"

The two kids fell silent as they dug through the junk. Mason's garage sale haul turned out to be much less exciting than Liam's. In fact, it was mostly spoons. Finally, Elsa reached the bottom of the box and dug out the old slime-filled lantern. "Aha!"

"Gotcha!" Mason shouted as he barged back into the garage with his dad. He pointed at Liam. "That's the kid who scratched your Tesla."

"Where's the scratch?" Mr. Farkas demanded.

"Right here on the . . ." Mason's voice trailed off. The scratch had disappeared. He looked at Liam. "What did you do with it?"

"There was never any scratch."

Mr. Farkas inspected the bumper, then turned back to the house. "If you pull this one more time . . ."

"Wait! Dad!"

Slam.

Mr. Farkas disappeared inside the house. Mason balled up his fists. "Give it back."

"Give what back?" Liam asked.

"The thing! The thing you just stole!"

"You mean the thing you stole from me?!"

Mason pushed Liam aside and growled at Elsa, "You're going to give that back."

Liam stepped back in front of Mason. "Or what?"

Liam only said that because it sounded like something a tough guy on TV would say. He didn't actually want to find out what Mason had planned. Fortunately, he wouldn't have to.

"Get him!" Tommy piped up. "He's a crumb!"

Everyone turned to Tommy. He'd just swallowed an alarming amount of gum to make this declaration.

"What did you call me?" Mason asked.

"Not you!" Tommy said. "Him! He's a crumb!"

"Me?!" Liam yelped.

Mason stood there with a goofy smile on his face for a second, then hooted with laughter. "That's perfect! A crumb!"

"A crumb BUM!" Tommy shouted, delighted at the attention he was getting.

"Ahahaha!" Mason laughed so hard that he was having a hard time breathing. "That's good," he finally said. "That's good stuff. You know what? I like you. You talk like a clown, you dress like a clown—I can respect that."

Respect. That single word turned Tommy into a grinning goofball. "Th—thanks, pal!" he stuttered as he reached out to shake the hand of his new best friend/hero.

Mason didn't shake his hand because he was staring at the giant lump in Tommy's pocket. "What's that?"

"Oh this?" Tommy pulled out the bronze Scottie dog. "Sleepy Barkis! Wanna know how I got it?"

Ding!

The muffled ding of the chaos meter rang from Elsa's backpack. Liam's face fell, but Elsa smiled. She'd just come up with Plan D. If everyone was going to do the opposite of what Elsa said, she might as well use that to her advantage. "Tommy, no!" she shrieked. "Don't let him see that!"

Tommy immediately handed the dog over to Mason.

"Take it back! TAKE IT BACK!" Elsa yelled hysterically.

Elsa's protests raised Mason's interest in Scottish terriers from zero to two-thousand percent. "Tell you what," Mason said. "I'll trade you the lantern for the dog straight up."

"NOOOOOO!"

"It—it would be an honor," Tommy stammered. For the second time, Tommy tried to shake Mason's hand. For the second time, Mason didn't shake.

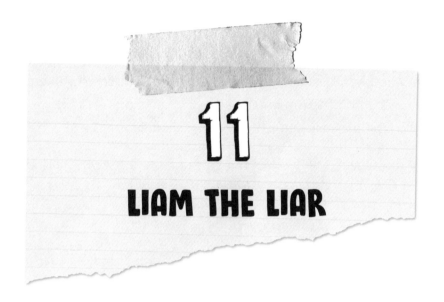

11

LIAM THE LIAR

"Why did you give that dog to him?" Liam asked Elsa as they biked back to Liam's house. "Didn't that raise the chaos meter?"

"Probably a little," Elsa replied. "But in ten minutes, it'll be gone anyway."

"What does that mean?" Tommy asked.

Elsa and Liam kept their mouths shut. They didn't need to give Tommy any reason to send the chaos meter into the yellow.

Back at Liam's house, Elsa started working in the basement, while Liam brought Tommy into the living room to keep him occupied. The TV was still on, although *Wheel of Fortune* had long since finished. Currently, an ad for fungus cream was playing on mute. Liam plopped onto the couch. "Want to watch TV?"

Tommy remained standing. "I want to rob a bank."

"You don't need to travel all this way to rob a bank when you can do that back in 1933. TV is one of the greatest things we have. Look." Liam switched the channel. Four people in a fancy studio were shouting over each other about tax cuts.

"See, they're not really in the TV," Liam explained. "They're recorded on cameras far away from here."

Tommy looked unimpressed.

"OK, so this probably isn't the best example." Liam switched to the sports channel.

"The Cowboys, as an organization, believe in their quarterback," a handsome man in a suit explained.

"But do you believe in their quarterback?" a nearly identical handsome man asked.

"I believe that injuries happen and . . ."

"DO YOU BELIEVE THAT HE'S A FRANCHISE QUARTERBACK—YES OR NO?!"

Liam gave Tommy a nervous smile. "Um, I promise there's more to it than this."

Tommy shook his head and marched downstairs. Liam clicked off the television and followed after him.

"What was all the yelling up there?" Elsa asked when they reached the bottom of the stairs.

"You said I could rob a bank," Tommy snapped.

"*He* said you could rob a bank." Elsa pointed at Liam with one hand, while swirling time slime inside the lantern with the other. "Liam, why don't you work on a nice list of banks for Tommy to rob while I do this."

"I wouldn't trust this lamebrain with my laundry list," Tommy shot back.

People had been talking down to Liam all day, and he'd remained pretty proud of himself for keeping it together. But Tommy picking up on Mason's nickname really bugged him. "Hey, what's your problem?"

"My problem?" Tommy asked. "You're the one who doesn't know how to use a time machine."

"Nobody knows how to use a time machine!"

"She does." Tommy pointed to Elsa, who was now studying the chaos meter and transferring drops of time slime from the lantern into a plastic cup.

"I am from the future, and I am smart," Liam said.

"You think you're smarter than me?" Tommy fired back.

"Yeah. I do. Cuz I know stuff that's gonna happen."

Tommy unscrewed a lightbulb from the ceiling and smashed it on the ground. "Did you know that was gonna happen?"

"Make him stop," Elsa said. "Every time he adds chaos, I have to remeasure the slime."

"You want chaos?" Tommy asked. "Bleeleeeleelee, woowoowoowoo, googityboogity!" He started spinning around the room and making faces. Liam grabbed Tommy's arm but couldn't hang on.

"Let him go," Elsa whispered. "That's not real chaos."

"WooOOOP! WooOOOP!" Tommy was now opening and closing his hands in front of his face and sticking out his tongue.

"Really?" Liam asked. "Because it looks like chaos."

"BONK! BONK! BONK! BONK!"

"He's just being weird; he's not actually changing anything in the real world. The chaos meter only moves when the real world changes."

Tommy stopped spinning. "But I am going to change the world. When I rob a bank."

Elsa kept her eyes on her work and her mouth shut.

Tommy stepped toward the workbench. "You said we were gonna rob a bank." He turned to Liam. "You PROMISED we were gonna rob a bank!"

Liam tried keeping quiet. He really did. But just like Mason with the Tesla, he couldn't help himself. "You can't rob a bank, OK?"

Tommy looked stunned.

Elsa tried giving Liam the signal to take it easy, but he continued anyway. "People don't run around robbing banks anymore. Cuz guess what? We have security cameras now! Lots of them!"

"We were never going to rob a bank, were we?"

"And they use exploding ink packets! And police helicopters! You know how I know that?!"

"You're a liar. Liam the Liar."

"I know that because I'm from the future, and I'm smart! You know what else I know?" Liam didn't need to continue. He'd already made his point and then some. But the words continued spilling out of his mouth anyway. "I know that

Tommy Twinkles is the worst gangster name in the history of the world."

"AHHHH!" Tommy jumped on top of Liam.

Liam had never been in a fight before. Never even thrown a punch. So he was totally unprepared for a scrap with Tommy Twinkles, a kid who probably punched people every day of his life.

"Elsa!" Liam screeched.

Elsa had just finished hooking the time machine's phone cord to the recombobulator. "Almost there!"

Wham! Wham! Wham!

Liam held his arms in front of his face while Tommy's fists slammed into him from every angle.

"Ready!" Elsa said. "Plug it in!"

Liam rolled toward the plug, which left his face open for a right hook.

SMASH!

Tommy landed a punch directly to Liam's jaw. Liam felt a crack.

Ding!

Liam was so disoriented by the blow that he didn't hear the chaos meter ring. Didn't know that it'd turned from green to yellow. He stumbled toward the power cord.

"Wait!" Elsa warned. "NO!"

Too late. Liam plugged in the time machine.

BLURP!

The machine sputtered to life. Then, it spit orange time slime all over the room.

Elsa ripped the recombobulator from the phone cord. "Unplug it!" she yelled to Liam.

Liam was too busy trying to rip Tommy off of his face to unplug anything.

Elsa ran over. "The meter went to yellow," she said as she tried ripping the cord from the wall. "It's not bringing back your parents!"

Thunk-thunk-thunk-thunk.

"What's—Ow—What's it—OUCH!" Liam tried asking a question while Tommy clawed at him like a badger.

"It's gonna bring other stuff from Tommy's time!" Elsa now held the power cord and pushed on the wall with both feet.

That got Tommy's attention.

"What stuff?" Tommy asked.

THUNK-THUNK-THUNK-THUNK.

Black smoke started billowing from the time machine. In addition to that smoke, purple cracks began forming in the wall.

"I don't know!" Elsa said. "Whatever was in the room with you right before you came here."

That spooked Tommy. He immediately dumped out a box, turned it upside down, and hid underneath it. Not a great sign.

Ka-CHUNK! Ka-CHUNK! Ka-ZZZZZZT!

Now, the time machine started flickering like a hologram.

Elsa glanced at the chaos meter. It was closing in on five. "Fuse box," she said.

"What?" Liam asked.

"WHERE'S YOUR FUSE BOX?!"

BBBBRRRRRR!

The time machine started revving like a jet engine and chugging so much black smoke that it was getting hard to see.

Elsa frantically searched the room. There, on the wall near the hot water tank, was a gray, metal box. Elsa ripped open the box's door to reveal a panel full of switches. She flipped every single one, turning off the power to the whole house. With no power, the time machine finally ran out of steam.

PUUUUUUuuuuuuuutz.

"Everyone OK?" Elsa asked in the dark.

Cough, cough.

"Hello?" Liam called. "Who's there?" He grabbed a flashlight from his dad's workbench and shined it around the room. All he could see was black smoke.

Cough, cough, wheeze.

Then, a figure emerged from the smoke. It wasn't Tommy. He was still hiding under a box. No, this was a full-grown man with the type of short mustache people grew before Adolf Hitler gave short mustaches a bad name.

Right beside him, another man emerged. He had a haircut like someone had stuck a bowl on top of his head, then taken a weed wacker to the rest of his hair.

Both of those guys were scary, but neither compared to the third man. He was thin and bony, with dead eyes and a crooked grin. Even though Liam had never met the man, he felt absolutely sure that he knew who this was. This was the world's scariest gangster.

This was Creepy Karpis.

12

CREEPY KARPIS AND THE BARKER BOYS

"What's the—*cough, cough*—what's the big idea?!" the mustache guy called out.

"I'm gonna turn the lights back on in three seconds, OK?" Elsa said.

"Who's that? Who said that?!" the bowl cut guy yelled.

"Wait," Liam said. "I don't think that's a good . . ."

"Three. Two. One."

Click.

"Baaarrgh!" all three men yelled. They covered their eyes and stumbled around. Mustache Guy started kicking the basement furnace.

Elsa didn't appear to be fazed by the chaos. She tried calming everyone down and said, "I know this may be confusing, but . . ." Bowl Cut Guy interrupted the speech by tripping over his own feet and toppling into her. She helped him up and continued in her museum tour guide voice. "Everyone please step this way."

Elsa was good at this. She'd clearly dealt with her fair share of discombobulated time travelers. Eventually, she wrangled all three men to the couch on the comfy-cozy side of the basement. Mustache Guy picked up one of the couch pillows and dropped it over and over like he was discovering gravity for the first time, while Bowl Cut Guy tugged on his face skin. But Liam kept his eye on Creepy Karpis. Karpis remained perfectly still, except for his eyes. He slowly scanned every inch of the basement.

"Gentlemen, I have some great news for you," Elsa said in an upbeat voice. "You've taken a trip to the future!"

"Is this Mars?" Mustache Guy asked.

"Great question! No, it's not Mars."

Bowl Cut Guy started smelling his armpits.

"That's not you," Elsa said. "You smell terrific!" (That was a lie. He smelled like beef jerky.) "That unusual odor is the result of time travel, and it'll clear up in just a few moments. In the meantime . . ." Mustache Guy raised his hand like he was in school. "Yes?" Elsa asked.

"Are you a Martian?"

Elsa smiled again, but this time it was more strained. "Maybe we should introduce ourselves. My name is Elsa. I'm a human girl."

"That's Creepy Karpis, and we're the Barker Boys," the mustache guy said. "We're human gangsters." He smiled, revealing a mouthful of crooked teeth.

"Wonderful!" Elsa said like that really was wonderful.

Bowl Cut Barker raised his hand, following the example of his brother. "What's that?" he asked, pointing to the TV.

"That's a television! I think you'll just love it." Elsa nodded to Liam. "Can you turn on the TV for our guests?"

"We don't have cable down here, so that's just for video games," Liam said.

"Then turn on video games for them," Elsa responded with a hint of annoyance in her voice despite the grin.

Liam fumbled with the remote, but he hadn't even hit the power button before Bowl Cut Barker walked to the entertainment center and pulled the TV off the stand, ripping cords out of the wall.

"Oh!" Elsa exclaimed. "Um, I like the idea, but that's not quite how you use it."

"We're stealing it," Mustache Barker said.

"OK! Sure! Go ahead!"

"We'll be stealing lots of this stuff."

"Of course! Knock yourself out!"

Liam leaned toward Elsa. "Can I have a word?" The kids retreated to the corner while the gangsters removed the "Home is where the love is" sign from the wall. "What are you doing?!" Liam hissed when he finally had Elsa alone.

"Keeping them calm."

"They're stealing my stuff!"

"Which is keeping them calm. Now, I need you to make sure everyone has a real nice time while I run a little errand . . ."

"You're leaving?!" Liam sputtered.

"You want your parents back, right? Then I need to get more time slime."

"But, but, but . . ."

"It'll just take a few minutes. They look very happy right now."

The bad guys did indeed look happy sorting through a box of old magazines.

"No matter what happens, just smile and . . ."

"YOU!" Mustache Barker growled when he picked up a box, revealing Tommy underneath.

Tommy tried crawling away, but the gangster grabbed his foot. "Hey, boss!" Mustache Barker yelled. "It's the kid! The kid who stole Sleepy!"

Everyone held their breath while Creepy Karpis walked toward Tommy. "Where's the dog?" he asked in a chilling tone.

"I—I don't have it!" Tommy said.

Creepy Karpis then swiveled to Liam and Elsa. "Where's the dog?"

At that moment, Tommy shook his foot free. "RUN!"

13

HOME ALONE

Liam and Elsa scrambled up the stairs, but Tommy wasn't so lucky. One of the Barker brothers dragged him back into the basement before he could reach the top.

"Hellllp!" Tommy screamed.

Liam and Elsa continued sprinting. They ran out the door to their bikes, then pedaled as fast as they could. Finally, Elsa pulled over. "We've got to go back."

"Those are gangsters!" Liam squealed. "Real-life gangsters!"

"The recombobulator's back there."

"But—but—but . . ." Liam glanced back. It was hard to see in the dark, but he couldn't spot anyone following them yet. "I think they're still in there."

"Then we have to lure them out, won't we?"

"OK, OK, OK." Liam nodded. "What do gangsters like? Cheetos?"

Elsa blinked a few times before responding. "You want to leave a trail of Cheetos? Like for a dog?"

"Got a better idea?"

"Yes. Literally any idea."

But after talking through ten progressively worse ideas, the kids came to the unfortunate conclusion that Cheetos were their best bet. Elsa ran home to grab the snacks and reassure her parents that things were A-OK over at the Chapmans. They didn't need to worry, even if this project took awhile.

"How many of those do you keep in your house?!" Liam marveled when Elsa returned with five party-sized bags of Flamin' Hot Cheetos.

"Hopefully enough."

They arranged all five bags in a neat pile next to the side door, then knocked.

Knock, knock, knock.

"Beat it!" a gravelly voice boomed from the basement.

Knock, knock, knock.

"It's those kids!" another voice said.

Clunk, clunk, clunk.

Someone was climbing the stairs! Liam and Elsa sprinted to the front of the house and hid around the corner. Elsa peeked and whispered running commentary.

"It's the Mustache Barker . . . he took the bait . . . he's eating, eating, eating . . . OK, here's his brother."

Liam strained to hear their crunching over the sound of his thumping heart. "What about Creepy Karpis?"

Elsa shook her head. "The first one just finished . . . he's going for bag number two . . . now the second one is done with his first bag."

Liam closed his eyes. The world's scariest gangster was in his house right now, and there wasn't a single adult he could call. Suddenly, his eyes popped open. He'd seen this exact scenario in a movie. And that gave him a solution. He started creeping toward the front door.

"Where are you going?" Elsa hissed.

"*Home Alone*," Liam whispered.

"Not alone!" Elsa whispered back. "There's one more!"

Liam shook his head and continued creeping. "The movie."

Elsa looked more confused than ever.

"*Home Alone* is a movie!" Liam tried to whisper from a distance too far for whispering. When that didn't work, he waved Elsa off and crept through the front door. Liam then turned on the living room TV and made sure it was muted. He clicked through the movies his family had recorded. Please, please, *please* let *Home Alone* be there.

Home Alone is a Christmas movie in which eight-year-old Kevin McCallister faces off against two home intruders. Every year, the Chapmans would watch young Kevin burn, tar, electrocute, and concuss the villains all in the name of holiday family fun. Liam wasn't interested in hurting his own home intruders, though. Instead, he needed the scene where Kevin tricks the bad guys into thinking someone's home by playing clips from a black-and-white gangster film. It's a great movie scheme that would never, ever work in the real world . . . unless someone were dealing with actual old-time gangsters.

Liam panicked when he reached the "H" movies, and *Home Alone* was missing. That panic only lasted a moment, though, because the Chapmans did have *Home Alone 2* recorded, and the gangster bit was so good in the first movie that the writers ran it back practically unchanged for the second movie. Liam fast-forwarded to the scene, turned the TV to full volume, then hit "play."

"I'm gonna give you to the count of three to get your lousy, lyin', low-down, four-flushin' carcass out my door!" the movie gangster shouted.

Liam listened for a sound from the basement. Silence.

"One!"

Nothing yet.

"Two!"

Still nothing.

Bang-bang-bang-bang!

The movie gangster started shooting and laughing like a maniac. "Hahahahaha!"

Clunk, clunk, clunk.

Yes! That was the sound of Creepy Karpis running up the basement stairs!

"Three. Merry Christmas, ya filthy animal," the movie gangster said before shooting a few more rounds. "And a happy New Year."

Elsa ran through the front door cackling. "They're falling all over each other out there!"

The kids sprinted downstairs, where they found Tommy tied up with an extension cord.

"You came!" Tommy cheered. "You came back for me!"

"Uhhh, yeah! Yeah, of course we did," Liam replied, despite temporarily forgetting about Tommy. He worked on Tommy's knots while Elsa disconnected the recombobulator from the time machine.

"Where's the bean shooter?" Tommy asked.

"The what?"

"The gun you were shooting up there."

"Oh no, that was a movie."

"Hm. That's a shame," Tommy said. "You might wanna get a real one."

Suddenly, Liam had a terrible thought. "Tommy, those guys aren't going after Mason, are they?"

Tommy shook his head proudly. "I ain't a stool pigeon! I didn't say one word about Mason. They think I have the dog, so they want to kill me."

Liam glanced nervously at Elsa. "How much longer is this going to take?"

Elsa shook her head and kept working.

"They say you can't outsmart Alvin Karpis," Tommy continued. "Pfff. Tommy Twinkles found him when the G-Men couldn't."

"Elsaaaa?" Liam called.

"And no one'll go near Fred and Doc Barker. Bloody Barkers, they call 'em." Tommy tugged on his suspenders with pride. "Like taking candy from a baby."

"ELSA!"

"Done." Elsa stuffed the recombobulator in her backpack and zipped it up. "Let's go."

Liam's stomach twisted in a knot. "Go where?!"

14
FRANKENSTEIN SANTA

"Where are we going?" Liam repeated as the kids walked up the stairs.

Elsa stuck her head out the side door and waited for her eyes to adjust to the dark.

"Yoohoo," Liam said. "Where are we going?"

"Sh," Elsa hushed Liam, then looked down the driveway.

"Cuz the time machine's right here!" Liam continued. "We can use it to go back and change everything we just did!"

"Not the way it works." Elsa leaned farther out the door to get a better glimpse of the street. "We caused chaos. Time slime is the only way to erase that." When Elsa saw that the gangsters were gone, she hopped on her bike.

Liam grunted his frustration as he motioned for Tommy to join him on his bike. The kids rode silently through the neighborhood, jumping every time a dog barked or light

flickered. Elsa finally stopped on Dellbrook Lane. She held her finger to her lips and scanned the area for a long time. Satisfied that they weren't being followed, Elsa continued to the end of the street and turned onto the bike path.

Liam's heart sank. Not the bike path. The Dellbrook Lane trail wound through the small forest surrounding their neighborhood, making it the perfect spot to spy chipmunks during the day or get murdered by time-traveling gangsters at night. To keep this very real possibility off his mind, Liam started talking to Tommy. "Hey. Sorry I said that about your gangster name. It's not that bad."

"It's the best gangster name," Tommy replied confidently.

"So—I agree, OK—but have you tried any others?"

"I've always been Tommy Twinkles."

"Right, but gangster names are usually tough and scary."

"Oh, you mean like Baby Face Nelson?" Tommy asked.

"Um . . ."

"Or Pretty Boy Floyd?"

Liam had never heard of those gangsters before, but he thought that they also needed better names.

"When I was little, Miss Malloy told me they'd put my name in lights one day. Big, twinkling lights. So that's why I'm Tommy Twinkles. And I'm not changing for no one."

"Who's Miss Malloy?"

"At the orphanage."

"Oh." Liam didn't know how to transition to another question from that, so he rode in silence for a bit. Tommy sniffed. Finally, Liam said, "Miss Malloy sounds pretty great."

"She was."

"Here," Elsa said. She turned off the path and ditched her bike next to a tree. Liam did the same. Elsa switched on her phone's tiny flashlight, which did little besides illustrate how big and dark and scary the forest actually was. They crept for awhile, then slid down a hill covered with dead leaves. It felt like the middle of the wilderness, at least until Tommy clanked into a pile of old cans.

Finally, the kids reached an iron fence with pointy posts. It looked super old and super hard to jump. Without hesitating, Tommy placed his hand on one of the flat posts, hopped up, then flipped his body over the fence. Elsa—not someone known for her athleticism—pulled off the same move. That gave Liam the confidence to try his own vault. After three failed attempts and a ripped shirt, Elsa and Tommy finally dragged Liam over the fence like a sack of wet laundry.

Once he made it over the fence, Liam figured out where he was. "Professor Snellenburg's," he whispered.

He'd seen pictures of the professor's backyard, of course. They were in the documentary. But he was still unprepared for how much of a mess it'd be. Even in the moonlight, he could see that the whole yard was filled with failed experiments too rusty to sell at the garage sale.

"Why didn't we just go through the front yard?" Liam asked.

"We couldn't risk anyone seeing us come here," Elsa said as she picked her way through the yard. "Not the gangsters, not the neighbors—no one."

Elsa finally reached a device that looked like it could either be a *Star Wars* droid or a pool filter. She twisted a knob until it popped off, shoved her hand down into the contraption, winced, then pulled out a skeleton key covered in black goo. She wiped the goo off on the ground, then led the way to the old-timey cellar with exactly the type of door that one would expect a goo-covered skeleton key to open.

CREEEAAAAAK.

Elsa opened the door and motioned for the boys to step down into the black pit. Once everyone had descended into the darkness, Elsa closed the cellar door and flipped on a light.

Liam had gotten so used to the dark that he had to shield his eyes. But when he opened them—whaaaaa . . .

Professor Snellenburg's cellar was half-Frankenstein's laboratory and half-Santa's workshop. There was all the obvious mad scientist stuff like triangle beakers, tubes that looped in circles, and a rusty hospital bed. But there was also a skateboard with a very tiny jet engine screwed to the back. There were stuffed animal heads on top of elaborate robot bodies. There were Nerf guns with unauthorized upgrades. Then, there was . . . was that a . . .

"Is this a real cat?!" Tommy asked, picking up a blue cat off the table.

"Put that back."

"Cuz it looks real. But it's blue." Just then, the cat's tail split open, revealing a spring.

"I said, put it back!"

Tommy carefully set it back on the table like he thought the rest of the toy might explode.

"Now, listen," Elsa said. "We're looking for more time slime. It should be—"

SLAP!

Elsa slapped Tommy's hand as he reached for a pile of disturbingly neon peppermints. "The time slime should be in milk cartons."

"Like this one?" Liam grabbed a carton from a box near his feet, then slumped his shoulders. "Oh. It's empty."

"No, it's not." Elsa took the carton from Liam's hand and shook it. Something sloshed inside. "It just feels empty because time slime is nearly weightless. Just look for more—I SAID, STOP!"

Tommy now held a half-dozen bouncy balls.

"Don't move." Elsa took the balls out of his hand and set them on a table as gently as she possibly could. "Those are super bouncy bouncy balls. If you drop them, then they will never, ever stop bouncing."

Tommy's eyes lit up. "I wanna try."

"You know what, I changed my mind." Elsa picked up the blue cat and pushed it into Tommy's arms. "Hold this cat. Make sure nothing happens to it. This is a very important job."

Tommy looked delighted to be trusted with such a vital task.

Then, Elsa pointed to Liam. "Find more time slime. Take as much as you can carry."

Liam nodded, turned, then fell on his face. He'd tripped over a crack in the concrete that extended the length of the cellar. One side of the crack had buckled up a few inches, creating a very trippable ridge. Down on the ground, Liam could almost make out a faint purple glow shining through the crack.

"What's this?" Liam asked.

Elsa ignored the question. "Hurry up. This cat thing won't distract him long."

Liam started digging through boxes. How much junk did this guy have? There were Thanksgiving placemats, half-used candles, a salad spinner, a . . .

Whoa.

Liam picked up a needlepoint that looked like it had been sewn decades ago. It showed a boy and girl in old-timey clothes, "Sweet is the morning of youth inspired by love and truth." The name under the boy was "Wolfgang." The name under the girl: "Elsa."

"Um, Elsa?" Liam asked.

Creak.

What was that noise? Elsa held her finger to her lips.

Creak. Creak. Crrreeeeeaaaaaak.

Tommy panicked and dove under a table, but Elsa motioned for everyone to relax. "No one followed us," she whispered. "I was watching the whole time."

Liam shook his head. Elsa liked to act like she had everything under control, but someone was clearly upstairs. He turned and ran up the cellar stairs toward the backyard. When he opened the door, a familiar face greeted him.

"Hello," Creepy Karpis said with a crooked grin.

15

NO FUNNY BUSINESS

Creepy Karpis marched Liam back down the stairs. "Come on down, boys!" he called.

The Barker brothers descended another staircase on the opposite side of the cellar. Elsa tried her smile again. "Hiiii, guys. Long time, no see!"

Bowl Cut Barker returned Elsa's fake smile with one of his own as he patted a chair. "Please step this way," he said, echoing Elsa's words from earlier.

While Elsa sat, Liam tried to bargain. "You liked those Cheetos? We know where to get more. Lots more!"

Mustache Barker roughly pushed Liam into another chair. The Barker brothers may have been thrown off their game when they time traveled to Liam's house, but now, they were in full intimidation mode.

When Liam sat, he made eye contact with Tommy, who was still hiding under the table. Liam tried pleading for help with his eyes. Tommy shook his head. He waited until Creepy Karpis turned his back, then slinked up the stairs before anyone saw him. Unbelievable! *This* was the thanks Liam got for saving Tommy earlier?

"We don't have Sleepy Barkis," Elsa said.

The Barker Boys were dumping boxes all over the cellar.

"That's the name of the dog, right? Sleepy Barkis? Cute name. I'm sure he was a cute dog. If you . . ."

"We don't care about that statue no more," Bowl Cut Barker interrupted.

Liam tried a different strategy. "You guys wanna see some cool future stuff? We can show you lots of future stuff. Like smartphones!"

The Barker Boys did not respond because they were too busy examining the one piece of futuristic technology that did interest them: duct tape.

"Oooh! You're gonna love the Apple Watch!" Liam continued. "So that's like a watch with a screen, not a real apple. I know that might be confus . . ."

RIIIIIP!

Mustache Barker ripped off a long strip of duct tape and used it to strap Liam to his chair. Bowl Cut Barker did the same to Elsa. Then, the gangsters dragged the kids' chairs to a table and nodded toward their boss.

Creepy Karpis dumped Elsa's backpack onto a table. Out fell the recombobulator, chaos meter, a jar of frosting, and a tin full of mints. Karpis popped a mint into his mouth and set the chaos meter on the table so both kids could see it. Then, he stood back with his arms folded.

Bowl Cut Barker stepped up. "Talk."

"OK, so the Apple Watch," Liam said. "It's like a Fitbit— actually, you probably don't have those either . . ."

Mustache Barker kicked Liam's chair. "Not you."

All eyes turned to Elsa. She cleared her throat. "That's part of a time machine."

"No kidding," Bowl Cut Barker replied. "How does it work?"

"How should I know? I'm just a kid."

Mustache Barker picked up a beaker, then smashed it so it had jagged edges. "You'd better figure it out. Kid."

If Elsa was scared, she didn't show it. "So what's the plan? You're gonna rob a bank, then go back in time?"

"We don't rob banks no more. Too messy."

"What do you do now?"

Creepy Karpis, who'd been silent to this point, smiled the creepiest smile someone could smile. "Kidnap."

Liam shivered. Now *this* guy had an appropriate gangster name.

"Congratulations," Elsa said. "You kidnapped us. Now what?"

"Well, we're gonna, uhhhh . . ." Mustache Barker was just now realizing that he didn't know what the plan was either, so he looked to his boss.

"Fix the time machine, and you'll live long enough to find out," Creepy Karpis said.

"Can't," Elsa said.

Mustache Barker took a threatening step toward Elsa.

"It's the World's Worst Time Machine. You saw that, right? It'll never take you where you wanna go. You don't need me to fix that time machine. You need me to build one."

Bowl Cut Barker chuckled.

"What? You don't think I know how to build a time machine?" Elsa leaned forward. "I'm from the future. Of course, I know how to build a time machine."

The Barker brothers looked at Creepy Karpis, who gave them a slight nod. Mustache Barker used the jagged beaker to cut through Elsa's duct tape. "No funny business," he warned.

"I'm her assistant!" Liam said. "You need me too."

The bad guys turned to Elsa for confirmation. She looked conflicted, then finally said, "No, I can do it myself."

SERIOUSLY?! Liam stared at Elsa with his mouth agape.

Elsa glanced in Liam's direction just long enough to mouth "sorry" before turning back to the gangsters. "Now, I'm gonna need you Barker Boys to help me find as many of these milk cartons as you can," Elsa tapped the time slime. "Can you do that?"

The Barkers gave her a weird look but reluctantly agreed.

Elsa then sorted through boxes until she pulled out a water pistol. Creepy Karpis watched her with a wary eye as she started tinkering with it.

Liam had no idea what Elsa's plan was, and he didn't care anymore. All he knew was that she'd abandoned him. First, his parents had been taken away, then Tommy ditched him, and now Elsa. He was alone. Completely alone.

Ding!

All eyes in the room snapped to the chaos meter. A purple ripple of energy pulsed from the clock as it struck six.

"What was that?!" Bowl Cut Barker shouted.

Liam was wondering the same thing.

Of course, no one was going to get a straight answer from Elsa. She tapped the water pistol and smiled. "That just means the time machine's almost ready!"

No, it actually meant that Tommy was somewhere in the world, causing chaos.

Liam spent the next half-hour staring at the chaos meter. Slowly, the needle marched toward seven. What could Tommy possibly be doing out there? Liam imagined him eating Cheetos and attempting robberies and getting arrested and ruining his chances of seeing his parents ever again. Finally, the meter hit seven.

Ding!

When that happened, purple light shot from the crack running through the cellar floor.

"WHAT WAS *THAT*?!" Bowl Cut Barker bellowed.

Creepy Karpis motioned for everyone to be quiet. He pointed to his ear. Liam didn't hear anything at first, but eventually, he could make out muffled voices outside.

"Stay here." Creepy Karpis grabbed Mustache Barker and marched up the stairs into the house. As soon as they left, the chaos meter started going crazy.

Ding-ding-ding-ding!

The needle suddenly jumped to the red zone. Purple sparks shot like fireworks from the cracks in the floor. The walls appeared to momentarily glitch. Bowl Cut Barker pounded on the chaos meter. "Make it stop!"

Liam and Elsa exchanged a terrified look. Was it broken? What could possibly be causing this much chaos?!

Clunk-clunk-clunk.

They got their answer a moment later when the two most chaotic people in the world tumbled down the stairs. Those people, of course, were Thomas Edison and Mason Farkas.

BOOF!

They tackled Bowl Cut Barker to the ground.

16 $z^{z^{z^z}}$

SWEET DREAMS

"Sweet dreams!" Mason taunted.

Mason was under the unfortunate impression that he'd knocked out Bowl Cut Barker by clunking his head on the ground. According to the movies, a simple blow to the head is enough to knock out even the toughest bad guy. That's almost never the way the real world works. In real life, clunking someone on the head just makes them furious. And Bowl Cut Barker was very furious.

"AHHHH!" The gangster leaped to his feet and grabbed Mason's shirt.

Tommy wasn't about to let his best friend in the whole world go down. He snatched one of the modified Nerf guns and pointed it at the ceiling to fire off a few warning shots. "EAT LEAD!"

Nerf guns, of course, do not shoot lead. This one didn't even shoot Nerf darts.

Pff—ff—ffff.

The gun sputtered a few puffs of pink gas. Unfortunately, it was not knockout gas or pepper spray. Even stinkbomb gas would have been helpful. No, this gas just carried the mildly unpleasant smell of bubble gum farts.

Tommy's attempted heroics did create enough confusion for Elsa to launch the real weapon: a fistful of bouncy balls. The balls all missed Bowl Cut Barker on their initial pass, but that didn't matter. Remember, these were not your standard-issue bouncy balls. They were super-bouncy bouncy balls. The balls ricocheted around the room, gaining speed with every bounce. Eventually, one found its target. And then another and another.

"Ow, ow, OW!" Bowl Cut Barker ducked and covered his head.

Elsa used the distraction to work on Liam's duct tape.

"Didja see who I got?!" Tommy proudly shouted while shielding his face.

"I had a plan," Elsa moaned, while being pelted by bouncy balls.

"Mason wasn't gonna come," Tommy continued. "Didn't believe me. But then, I showed him this!" He held up the blue cat by its springy tail.

"Leave the cat. Leave Mason," Elsa said.

Tommy shook his head. "Mason is a hero."

Mason didn't look particularly heroic at the moment. He was huddled on the ground holding his rear end, which had just suffered a direct blow from a super-bouncy bouncy ball.

"Also," Tommy added, "He brought Sleepy."

Just then, Creepy Karpis and Mustache Barker burst into the room.

"That's the guy!" Tommy yelled to Mason.

Mason had no intention of simply handing over Sleepy Barkis. No, he was about to become a hero. Mason gritted his

teeth, pushed through the pain, sprung to his feet, and cocked the bronze dog behind his head. In the hands of a trained action hero, the pooch was the perfect size and weight to knock someone out.

"SWEET DREAMS!" Mason screamed as he threw the statue as hard as he could at Creepy Karpis.

It missed by three feet.

Creepy Karpis picked Sleepy up off the ground and took a moment to smile at the statue. Then he set it down and calmly started walking toward Mason.

"Whoa, whoa, whoa!" Mason backed up.

"Hurry," Liam whispered to Elsa.

Creepy Karpis continued his steady march. Super-bouncy bouncy balls pelted the gangster's face and chest, but they didn't appear to bother him one bit.

"You don't think I came to rescue these guys, do you?" Mason asked as he continued backpedaling. "Because you can have them. This clown didn't even tell me they were here."

Bowl Cut Barker grabbed Mason to keep him from backing up farther. Liam couldn't watch.

Mason switched strategies. "If you hurt me, my dad will make you pay! He's a LAWYER!"

Creepy Karpis paused, which made Mason smirk. "Thaaaat's right," Mason continued. "A big, powerful lawyer."

There was a moment of silence as the gangsters exchanged a look. Finally, Mustache Barker asked, "This lawyer got money?"

"More than you can imagine. He drives a Tesla."

That's exactly what the gangsters wanted to hear. (Minus the Tesla part. They didn't know what that was.) This kidnapping was going to make them rich.

"Tie him up," Creepy Karpis commanded.

Ding!

The chaos meter struck nine.

GGGGRRRRRR.

Something underground made a sound so deep that everyone felt it in their bones. The Barkers looked scared for a moment, but their concern ended as soon as the sound did. Mustache Barker prepared a chair, while Bowl Cut Barker dragged Mason toward it.

"No! Stop!" Mason struggled and kicked and squirmed to no avail.

"He said STOP!" Tommy shouted.

Everyone turned toward Tommy. He was standing on the jet engine skateboard, holding the water pistol Elsa had been working on earlier. Bowl Cut Barker smirked. Mason looked disappointed. The only person who gave Tommy his desired reaction was Elsa.

"NO!" she screamed.

Of course, Tommy didn't listen to Elsa. No one ever listened to Elsa. He pulled the trigger.

KAPOOOOMF!

The water pistol did more than wheeze a few puffs of gas. A lot more. Dense pink foam exploded from the gun, filling the room from floor to ceiling. The blast was so strong that it temporarily deafened everyone. It knocked Tommy on his back. It shook the whole house. And it shattered the recombobulator into a million pieces.

THE BUTTON

The foam wall sealed off Liam, Elsa, and Tommy from the rest of the room. It trapped Mason with the gangsters, which gave Elsa enough time to cut Liam out of his chair. When she finished, she grabbed the chaos meter and headed up the stairs to the backyard. Tommy tried hacking through the foam to rescue Mason, while Liam picked tiny recombobulator pieces off the ground.

"Guys! Now!" Elsa hissed.

"But . . ." Liam and Tommy both said in unison.

"It's too late," Elsa replied.

It was too late. Too late for Mason. Too late for Liam's parents. Too late for a normal life ever again. Liam and Tommy reluctantly joined Elsa in running up the cellar stairs, through the backyard, and into the forest.

Liam didn't cry until they reached the bikes, but once he started—hoo boy, did he sob. It was a shoulder-shaking, can't-breathe panic cry so intense that even Tommy could see he needed to keep his mouth shut. Elsa had seemed so sure of herself all night that Liam never once seriously considered the possibility that his parents might be gone forever. And then, with one blast from a stupid Nerf gun, his world came crashing down. Liam was an orphan now, just like Tommy.

Ding!

As if to emphasize just how dire the situation was, the chaos meter chose this moment to strike ten. A purple bolt streaked across the sky, and the ground quaked. Trees got all blocky like they were in an old video game before returning to normal.

Liam blamed a lot of people for this mess. He blamed Mason. He blamed himself. Tommy, obviously. Elsa laid a hand on Liam's back. He swatted it away. "This is your fault!" he shouted.

"Liam . . ."

"No! You wouldn't talk to me before. Don't talk to me now."

"I . . ."

"Why don't you trust me? Huh? What did I ever do to you?!" The bitterness pushed aside the tears for a moment. Good. Liam embraced it. "I could've helped back there! Could've helped all night! But you left me tied up, and you left me in the dark, and, and, and just tell me what I did to you, OK?! Cuz I thought we . . . I thought we were . . ." Liam started crying again once his rant lost steam.

Elsa gave him a moment before whispering, "I just wanted to say that I know how you feel."

"No, you don't," Liam mumbled.

Elsa sat on the cold, wet ground next to Liam. It was too dark to get a good look at her face, but the sniffing coming from her direction told Liam that she was crying too. For awhile, everyone remained quiet. Then, Elsa said, "You probably figured out that Professor Snellenburg was my grandpa, huh?"

Liam didn't answer, and Elsa didn't seem to care. She continued talking like she'd been bottling something up for a long, long time. "He was, um, he was an inventor, obviously. Everyone knows that. But most people don't know that he started as a toy inventor. That's, like, a real job. The big toy companies get their ideas from toy inventors all over the world. I didn't know that 'til pretty recently."

Liam didn't know that either, and he certainly didn't care. He was gearing up to yell at Elsa again, but she continued before he could start speaking.

"I guess when my mom was little, one of the big companies stole some of my grandpa's ideas. Then, they threatened him and stuff. I don't know the whole story, but it made my grandpa super-duper secretive about everything. Then, my grandma died, which made him even more secretive and sad."

"Sorry," Liam mustered.

"My parents thought it'd be a good idea for me to stay with him for a month or two the summer after my grandma died to cheer him up. I was always his favorite. He called me his 'little button.' I'm not sure why. I guess cuz he liked buttons? Anyways, a few days after I arrived, he showed me the time machine."

Tommy sat on the ground too. He sensed the story was about to get good.

"The time machine didn't work when I got to his house. It was just a bunch of wires and old junk. Honestly, it looked like he'd gone a little crazy. But once I showed up, it started to work."

"You fixed it?" Tommy asked.

"I didn't fix anything. It just always seemed to work whenever I was around. My grandpa rebuilt the machine a million times in a million different ways. No matter what he did, the machine worked when I was around, and failed when I left. He said I was the missing piece."

Liam was trying to act disinterested, but his eyes widened when he remembered something. "'Little button' was the last step in the instructions."

Elsa nodded. "I'm the button."

"But I got it to work when you weren't in my basement."

"Right. Because I'm not the missing piece," Elsa said. "Belief is."

Liam would believe just about anything, but this sounded silly even to him. "Uh, OK."

"No, really! The machine will almost always work no matter how you put it together. Sometimes you have to jiggle a few loose wires, sometimes you have to add more power, but you can usually get it to work if you believe it'll work. I know that sounds corny, but it's true. That's why it works for kids, but not adults. And that's why I was so important to my grandpa. Any time he stopped believing, even for a second, he could count on me to keep him safe."

Except, Professor Snellenburg was no longer safe. Which meant Elsa must have failed.

"The few weeks that the time machine worked were the greatest of my life. We traveled all over the world and all over time. The machine still messed up here and there, but whenever things would start to go wrong, we'd run the recombobulator and fix them. We never let the chaos meter get anywhere near twelve—never even let it get to the yellow."

"So what happened?" Tommy asked.

"I—I, uh . . ." Elsa took a deep breath. "So I think that . . ." She stopped talking. Liam stared at the ground waiting for her to start back up again, but all he heard was the sound of crickets chirping. He finally looked over to see Elsa's face buried in her hands and her shoulders shaking.

"It's OK," Liam whispered. "You don't have to tell us."

"I don't think I can," Elsa said. Then, she looked up. "But maybe I can show you."

18
THE PIT

Elsa led the gang back to Liam's house, then did a quick check for intruders before shuffling down to the basement. She picked up the headlamp Liam had used to project his memories earlier and took a deep breath. "I never thought I'd show this to anyone." Then, she plugged the time machine's telephone cord into the headlamp port and closed her eyes.

Soon, a projection appeared on the wall. It showed a younger version of Elsa walking out of Professor Snellenburg's front door.

"You live here?" a voice asked.

The camera zoomed out to reveal a wide-eyed woman on the sidewalk with a bunch of camera equipment. She wore a University of Missouri t-shirt and struggled with all the gear. It looked like she might be working on her first big project out of college.

"I'm, uh, just getting the mail," Elsa replied.

"Does the professor live here?" the woman asked. "I was hoping to talk to him for a documentary."

Elsa shook her head. "He doesn't like to talk about his work."

"Oh, for sure! I mostly just wanted to tell him what a big fan I am."

"I'll let him know."

"It would mean a lot for me to be able to tell him in person," the woman said with a hint of desperation in her voice. "Is he home right now?"

Elsa paused, then nodded. "But he's working on something right now. Maybe another day."

The woman's eyes lit up. "A new project?"

Elsa smiled. "A *big* project." With that, she grabbed the mail and walked back to the house. The video ended there.

Liam looked from the blank wall to Elsa's face. Her eyes were all red. Was he missing something? Liam was expecting some deep, dark secret, and instead, all he witnessed was a moment of politeness. "Um, was that the right video?" he finally asked.

"My grandpa had one rule: don't talk to anyone."

"Yeah, but you didn't."

"I told her that he was working on something big."

"That doesn't mean anything."

"Nothing causes chaos faster than talking. My grandpa said that over and over and over. Remember what I told you earlier? You can control what you say, but you can't control what anyone else says."

"But you didn't say anything!" Liam sputtered. He felt like he needed confirmation that he wasn't crazy, so he turned to Tommy. Unfortunately, Tommy had already checked out of the conversation. He'd kept the blue cat from the professor's cellar, and he was now bouncing it up and down by its spring tail like a yo-yo.

"Sometimes what you say doesn't matter as much as who you say it to," Elsa explained. "I don't know who this woman is, but she did something that night that caused chaos. A lot of chaos." Elsa closed her eyes again, and an image of her sleeping projected onto the wall. She slept soundly until the bed started rumbling. Her eyes popped open.

"Grandpa?"

The whole room was shaking.

"Grandpa?!"

She scrambled out of her bedroom. Pictures fell off the wall. A nightstand tumbled over. When she reached the hallway, a faint ringing sound joined the rumble. Elsa sprinted downstairs. The ringing got louder. Then, she flung open the cellar door. A purple glow hit her face.

"GRANDPA!"

The cellar lab looked like a scene from a horror movie. The floor had cracked wide open into a pit so deep that it looked like it went down to the center of the earth. An eerie purple light pulsed from the depths of the pit.

"GRAAANDPAAA!"

No answer. The only sound was a constant ringing. Elsa ran down the stairs and picked up the chaos meter. It had struck midnight.

"No! Wait!"

Elsa dove for the time machine, which was teetering on the edge of the pit. She fumbled with the telephone cord, then searched for the recombobulator. While she tore apart the cellar, the rumbling stopped. The ringing turned off. The purple glow faded, and the pit started healing itself.

Elsa finally hooked up the recombobulator and poured in time slime. Once her supply ran out, she dragged over a blue barrel and dumped it, too. Orange goo glopped all over the machine, but nothing happened. Now that the pit had swallowed the source of the chaos, all the time slime in the world couldn't rewind time.

Finally, Elsa fell on the ground and started sobbing. Alone. The last image Liam saw before Elsa let the memory fade was a yellow University of Missouri lanyard on the ground.

"What did you do?" Liam asked softly.

"I tried to go back. I tried so hard to go back."

The headlamp showed Elsa struggling with the time machine. The machine zapped her into a series of increasingly nightmarish scenes. Some sent her into maze versions of Professor Snellenburg's home. Others were filled with flashing lights and dark tunnels. At least one had a shadowy creature. But it refused to take her back to her grandpa.

"Then, I tried to get help," Elsa continued.

The headlamp showed Elsa talking to police, parents, and neighbors about the time machine. No matter what she said—

no matter who she told—the scene always ended the same way. The adult would get zapped by the time machine, and Elsa would use the recombobulator to rewind time and bring them back.

"Finally, I gave up."

The headlamp displayed one final sad scene. In this one, Elsa packed everything into a box, labeled it "World's Worst Time Machine," then buried it under a tarp in the garage. She'd given up.

When the projector turned off, Elsa breathed a long, deep sigh. She'd carried that story alone for too long. "I couldn't tell my parents about the time machine, but I did tell them about the girl with the camera. I showed them the lanyard she left behind. They've been trying to find her ever since. That's why they moved to the neighborhood, and that's why they ran the garage sale today. They want her to come back because she's the only link to my grandpa."

"But they never found her?" Liam asked.

Elsa shook her head. "I think both the girl and my grandpa are gone forever."

Everyone sat quietly for a full minute. Finally, Tommy spoke up. "I'm real sorry about your grandpa. Seems like he was a swell guy."

Elsa nodded. "He is swell."

More silence. Then, Liam asked, "Do we need the recombobulator?"

"What?"

"You said the machine runs on belief. What if we believe hard enough? Can we still rewind time?"

Elsa shook her head. "You can probably get by without the recombobulator, but you absolutely need time slime to heal chaos. And now that the chaos meter is red, we'd need barrels of it, not cartons."

Liam's eyes widened. "Blue barrels!"

"What?"

"The time slime barrels! They're blue, right?"

"Yeah, they're blue," Elsa replied. "But they're long gone by now."

"Right," Liam said. "And I know who has them."

19

ABNORMAL, PARANORMAL, SUPERNORMAL

"Cats are spies," Liam declared.

"Excuse me?" Elsa asked.

"So there was a guy who thought cats are spies . . ."

"Cats are spies?!" Tommy looked down in horror at the blue cat in his hand.

"No," Liam answered. "At the garage sale today, there was a guy who thought that cats are spies. Elsa, he was telling your mom that he'd bought blue barrels. And he'd tried to drink from them."

"He tried to WHAT?!" Elsa exclaimed.

"Look him up!" Liam said. "If we find him, we find the time slime!"

Elsa searched "Cats Are Spies" on her phone.

"That's Google," Liam explained to Tommy. "It knows the answer to any question you could ask."

"Like how many birds there are in the world?" Tommy asked.

"What?"

"How many birds are living in the world right now? Ask it that."

"Why?!"

Tommy shrugged. "Something I've always wanted to know."

"It's—it's not going to know that," Liam stammered. "But anything else."

Elsa shook her head. "I'm not finding anything on this guy."

"Something else Googoo doesn't know," Tommy muttered.

"It's Google!" Liam grabbed Elsa's phone. "Let me try."

Unfortunately, the type of person who distrusts cats is also deeply suspicious of the World Wide Web. The cat guy didn't have a website or anything. Liam deflated for a moment before remembering one final lead. He dug through his pockets and pulled out the crumpled pamphlet Mrs. Rutledge had picked up off the ground at the garage sale.

The pamphlet, titled "Temporal Rifts and You," showed a spaceship flying out of a poorly Photoshopped crack in outer space. The bottom of the pamphlet read "Presented by MAPSI."

"Look up MAPSI," Liam told Elsa.

Google revealed that "MAPSI" was an abbreviation for Midwest Abnormal, Paranormal, and Supernormal Investigators. It also revealed that the members of MAPSI were absolute marketing geniuses compared to Cat Guy. Now, that doesn't mean their marketing was effective. They had fewer Instagram followers than most pets. But that wasn't for lack of trying. MAPSI tried so, so hard to get a following by posting nonsense every single day. Some days, they shared indecipherable chalkboard equations. Other days, they shared indecipherable rants about planet alignments. Occasionally, they got cute and shared indecipherable *Star Trek* memes.

Today was a banner day for MAPSI as several of its members appeared to have gathered at Professor Snellenburg's garage sale. There were pictures of the line stretching down Dearborne Avenue, the burnt circle on Professor Snellenburg's front lawn, and excited nerds posing in front of the famous house. But the final post—shared just five minutes ago—held the most promise.

"Click that," Liam said.

The caption said. "Freaks and geeks unite! Tonight, we party." Just like every other post, the party had zero likes. Elsa swiped through the pictures. Liam recognized several figures from the garage sale. Then, he gasped. "I think that's him!"

"Who?"

"The guy with wild eyes."

"They're all guys with wild eyes!"

Elsa swiped to the next picture. Then, it was her turn to gasp. This picture showed the whole group posing in front of the Discount Inn and Suites on Engle Road. All the men had gathered in front of the alien bus holding their garage sale finds. Right there in the center were three blue barrels.

"Tommy," Liam said. "Want to rob a Discount Inn and Suites?"

20
CATS ARE SPIES

Tommy thought about the offer for a moment, then shook his head. "I want to rescue Mason."

"This is how we rescue him," Elsa replied.

Tommy gave her a skeptical look.

"Look, we can't storm the cellar again. They'll be ready for us. But if we gather enough time slime, we can get Mason back to his house and send the gangsters back to 1933."

Tommy continued his skeptical look.

Liam joined the plea. "It's Mason's only chance. You've gotta trust us."

Tommy slowly nodded. "OK. Let's steal some slime."

Liam breathed a sigh of relief and sat the gang down on the couch to work out a plan.

"This has to be an in-and-out thing," Elsa began.

"Like ninjas or spies," Liam agreed.

"We bust in and tell 'em Tommy and the Kids are here," Tommy suggested.

"We'll need disguises," Elsa said.

"Or sneak in through the vents," Liam mused.

"First, we rough up the biggest guy to show them we mean business," Tommy continued.

"The barrels are big," Elsa said, "So we'll need a distraction."

"Wait, how are we going to carry them?" Liam asked.

"'Course, we'll need a chest full of choppers," Tommy added.

"Time slime barely weighs anything, remember?" Elsa asked. "My dad has a baby bike trailer he uses to tow around my little brother. That should work. I'll grab it from our garage before we go."

"It's important to surround the getaway car with hostages so the cops don't shoot," Tommy said.

"When we get home . . . I'm sorry, what?!" Liam had been tuning out Tommy this whole time, but that last sentence was so ridiculous that it got through his filter.

"The hostages stand outside the getaway car. You know, on the running boards. That way no one shoots during the getaway."

Elsa, who was used to Liam spouting nonsense all the time on the bus, calmly said, "Cars don't have running boards anymore."

"And also, why would we ever do that?!" Liam asked.

Tommy shrugged. "That's how John Dillinger does it."

"We're not John Dillinger! And you shouldn't want to be either."

"Why not?" Tommy asked. "He's rich. Everyone loves him."

"Because he gets caught! They all get caught."

"Really? How?"

"Well . . . So . . ." Liam faltered. "I mean, of course they get caught!"

"Hm," Tommy said, pleased with himself for winning the argument.

"Hey." Elsa tapped the chaos meter with its needle firmly in the red zone. "Let's go."

Elsa ran back to her house to sneak the bike trailer out of her garage, Tommy went to Liam's room to pick out clothes, and Liam hid the time machine in the basement closet just in case the bad guys returned.

Ten minutes later, Elsa met up with Tommy in Liam's bedroom. He was wearing a hoodie backwards. "Where's Liam?" she asked.

"He's downstairs looking at the Googoo thing," Tommy replied.

"LIAM!" Elsa yelled.

"Sorry." Liam jogged up the stairs with his dad's phone in his hands. "Didn't hear you come in."

"We don't have time for you to be playing games or whatever." Elsa threw the phone on the bed. "Now, let's get dressed."

The kids dressed up in waitstaff clothes—white shirts and black pants—for two reasons. First, spies always dress as waiters when they're trying to sneak into fancy parties, and the Discount Inn and Suites website said that MAPSI would be in Ballroom A, which sounded very fancy. Second, Tommy insisted that all the great gangsters wear suits for their robberies, and this was the best compromise. The kids all dressed in Liam's clothes, Elsa slung the backpack over her shoulder, and they set off into the night.

As the gang biked to the hotel, they came up with an elaborate cover story to get past the front desk. They would claim to be replacement caterers for the MAPSI party, as the original catering team had fallen ill due to food poisoning (bad enchiladas). If the hotel clerk mentioned that they looked too young to be caterers, the kids would credit their youthful appearance to a healthy diet (mostly kale and nutritional supplements). When the hotel would try verifying their names against the guest list, Liam would overwhelm them with a sales pitch for the nutritional supplements (antioxidants to slow aging, probiotics for gut health, and an exciting rewards program for joining the NutriWOW family).

None of that would be necessary.

The front desk clerk had seen way, way too much during her career at Discount Inn and Suites to raise an eyebrow at three kids scuttling through the lobby at 10 p.m., even three kids who scuttled as suspiciously as Elsa, Liam, and Tommy did. Once the kids made it to the door of Ballroom A, they realized that they hadn't come up with a real plan for stealing the time slime barrels. So they ducked into the indoor pool area (which was still conveniently open for another half hour thanks to the hotel's Swim Greater Later promotion) to come up with a new plan.

They decided that Liam would pick up empty appetizer trays and circle the ballroom once. He was to locate the cat guy, the time slime barrels, and a food service cart big enough to smuggle the barrels. If anyone asked what he was doing, he was to promise that the executive chef had some real tasty cheese plates coming right up. If someone asked why he looked so young—NutriWOW. He'd end his recon mission by wheeling a food service cart over to the pool area, where he'd load Tommy underneath the tablecloth.

None of that would be necessary.

"Ballroom" turned out to be an extremely generous label for the small space with tired wallpaper and stained carpet that hosted MAPSI. Also, there was no catering, no tablecloths, and no appetizers. Only a bunch of pasty, balding men surrounded by garage sale junk and empty pizza boxes. Liam may not have fit into the scene, but nobody seemed to care. Finally, there was no need to spy because the barrels were right there at the front of the room, and the Cats Are Spies guy was easily identifiable by his CATS ARE SPIES t-shirt. Liam reported back to the pool area.

"It's not gonna work," he said. "The room is too small and the barrels are right there for everyone to see. Maybe if we knock out the power grid and climb into the ceiling . . ."

"No more complicated plans," Elsa interrupted. "I'll distract, and you two grab the barrels. Act confident, and no one will say anything."

Liam wasn't too sure about that idea. Tommy was overly sure. "I'm confident," Tommy said as he stuck out his chest and strode toward the ballroom.

Elsa stepped in front of Tommy before he could cause a scene. She slipped into Ballroom A and quickly located Cat Guy. "Excuse me," she said. "I couldn't help but notice your shirt, and I was wondering why . . ."

"The media has spent hundreds of years conditioning you to believe that cats aren't spies!" the man exploded. He'd clearly been waiting for someone to ask him about his shirt all night. "They say that cats can't be trained. Do you know what a load of crock that is?!"

Tommy reached for a barrel, but Liam stopped him. The guy was still looking in their direction.

"You can train any common tabby cat to walk backward in under two hours. That's two hours! Now, if you don't think they're capable of a lot more than that after decades of CIA training, you're lying to yourself."

Liam squeezed Tommy's shoulder. *Wait. Waaaiiit.*

The guy stepped closer to Elsa and lowered his voice. "One time I saw . . ." His eyes locked on Elsa's backpack. "What's that?"

"Oh this? It's just . . ."

The guy blinked a few times. His paranoia was kicking in. "Wait, why are you here? Who are you?!"

Elsa flashed her biggest smile. "I'm just interested in learning the truth."

"Spy." His eyes darted around the room.

"What? No, I . . ."

"Spy!" he repeated louder.

A few weary eyes turned toward the scene. Elsa could see that she was starting to lose control of the situation, so she started her retreat. "I'm so sorry."

"Wait!" Cat Guy grabbed Elsa's backpack as she turned.

"Go!" Liam hissed as he picked up a barrel. Tommy grabbed one too.

Elsa's backpack ripped open, and two items popped out: the chaos meter and a blue cat with a spring for a tail.

"AAAAHHHH!" Cat Guy let out a blood-curdling scream that stopped everyone in the room. Everyone, that is, except for Liam and Tommy.

21 T.E.

END OF DAYS

Liam and Tommy did not make it out of the Discount Inn and Suites with their time slime barrels. Didn't even make it out of Ballroom A.

"THOSE ARE MINE!" Cat Guy screamed.

The members of MAPSI blocked Liam and Tommy's path. "Who are you?" one of them growled.

Most adults would dismiss Liam and Tommy as just a couple of kids fooling around, but not MAPSI. This was abnormal behavior—maybe even supernormal behavior—which meant the investigators were on the clock.

"Um, uh, so you see," Liam stuttered. "The caterers ate bad enchiladas, and . . ."

"You!" Cat Guy interrupted. "You were at the garage sale!"

"HEY!"

All eyes turned to the door. The woman from the front desk was standing there with her arms folded. "Quiet hours began at 10," she scolded. "If you're going to disturb the other guests, I'll send you back to your rooms right now!"

"But we have the ballroom 'til midnight," someone whined.

"Then you'd better behave 'til midnight."

"THEY ARE SPIES!" Cat Guy yelled.

The desk clerk huffed and looked at the kids. "Are you spies?" she asked sarcastically.

"No, ma'am," Liam answered.

She threw up her hands. "They say they're not spies. My hands are tied."

Tommy smirked. That was a mistake.

The clerk glared at Tommy. "But they are trespassers, and they need to return to their rooms immediately. Do I need to find your parents?"

"No, ma'am," Elsa answered.

The clerk harrumphed and returned to her desk.

"THEY ARE SPIES!" Cat Guy guy yelled after her.

"Ernie, stop. You're embarrassing yourself," said a guy wearing an embarrassing "2012: End of Days" t-shirt.

"Baaah!" Cat Guy retorted. "That's you! Cuz you're a sheep! Bah, bah, bah!"

Liam couldn't focus on the rest of the argument because he was too busy staring at the chaos meter lying on the floor. Despite all the chaos over the last minute, it hadn't moved a single tick. Elsa noticed the meter, too. And that gave her an idea.

"Can I tell you guys a secret?" she asked the room. That stopped the argument immediately. MAPSI loved secrets. Elsa pointed at Liam. "The hotel lady won't be able to find his parents. Do you know why? They got sucked into a time machine three hours ago."

Liam's eyes nearly popped out of his head.

"And this one over here? He can't call his parents either. They died a hundred years ago."

The End of Days guy fumbled with his phone to record this historic moment. The rest of MAPSI followed his example.

"She's kidding!" Liam said. "Totally kidding!"

Elsa jabbed Liam with her elbow and nodded toward the chaos meter. Its needle still hadn't moved. "Tommy, why don't you tell them your name?" Elsa said.

"Tommy Twinkles."

"That's not your real name, though, is it?"

"I don't like my real name."

"Tell 'em anyways, Tommy. In case they've heard of you."

"Thomas Edison," Tommy said.

A gasp rippled through the crowd. Still, the chaos meter remained steady.

"That's not the real Thomas Edison!" a voice yelled from the back of the room. "They're messing with us!"

"Not the real Thomas Edison?!" Tommy squealed as he pushed his way toward the voice. "You've got some nerve! Check your peepers, pal, cuz you're looking at the real orange peel!"

"Meet Thomas Edison, A.K.A. Tommy Twinkles," Elsa said. "He's from 1933. Tommy may not have invented the light bulb, but I just watched him clear out a room full of real-life gangsters. He's brave, strong, and tougher than any kid I know. Tommy loves Cheetos and hates crumbs."

"You're all crumbs!" Tommy shouted at the room.

"Tommy is capable of saying or doing anything at any time. Which makes him more dangerous than you can imagine." Elsa picked up the chaos meter and held it above her head for all to see. "This belonged to Professor Snellenburg. It's a chaos meter. When it hits 12, a temporal rift will open in this very room and swallow everyone alive. Just like it swallowed the professor."

Elsa paused to let that sink in. Members of MAPSI exchanged nervous glances. Perhaps no one in the world took temporal rifts as seriously as this crew.

"The meter is already at ten," Elsa continued. "And there's no telling what chaos Tommy might cause next." She nodded at Tommy, who did not pick up on the signal at all. But Liam did.

MAPSI was scared. They just needed one final push. A little fake chaos might do the trick.

"Bleeleeleelee," Liam started opening and closing his hands in front of his face and sticking out his tongue like Tommy had in his basement.

Now, Tommy got it. He joined the fun. "Googityboogity-googityboogity!" he yelled while spinning in circles.

"BagaWOOGA! BagaWOOGA!" Elsa flailed her arms over her head and got in the face of Mr. End of Days.

MAPSI had seen enough. "AHHHHH!" The men all screamed and stumbled over each other as they ran for the exit. Ballroom A cleared in record time.

When the kids finally had the room to themselves, they cheered. "We did it!" Liam shouted.

"But how?!" Tommy asked.

Elsa smiled and grabbed one of the blue barrels. "Because they've been talking nonsense for so long that no one actually listens to them anymore. You can't cause real chaos if the world ignores you. When I saw how the front desk lady acted when they told her we were spies, I realized that we could tell them the truth, and it wouldn't make a difference."

Tommy winked at Elsa. "You're pretty smart, toots."

"Don't call me 'toots.'"

The kids rolled all three barrels out of the hotel's rear exit. The barrels were much too big for the bike trailer, but Elsa secured them all thanks to some creative bungee cording. The kids pedaled slowly back to Liam's house to keep the barrels from falling, while keeping a wary eye out for conspiracy theorists and gangsters. So far, the chaos meter remained stuck at 10. So far, the plan was working.

Back home, Liam sprinted to the basement and pulled out a key. "I locked the time machine in this closet." When he reached the closet, though, he paused. Orange fingerprints covered the door. Those weren't there earlier.

"Open it!" Tommy said.

Liam backed up. Something was wrong. He glanced toward the scary side of the basement. The lights were off. He hadn't turned them off earlier, had he? With his heart beating through his chest, Liam crept over to the scary side and turned on one of the bulbs.

There was the time machine, all assembled and ready to go. There was bronze Sleepy Barkis, sitting proudly on the workbench. And there, waiting with Cheeto crumbs all over his mouth, was Creepy Karpis.

"I've been expecting you."

22

MAN OF GENIUS

Creepy Karpis stood and stretched. "Why do you think they call me Creepy Karpis?" he asked. The kids were too shocked to answer, so the gangster tried again. "Don't be scared," he said with a scary grin. "Why do you think they call me Creepy Karpis?"

"Your, um, smile?" Elsa finally guessed.

Creepy Karpis smiled even wider. "You think my smile's creepy?"

"It's not your smile," Liam answered quietly. "It's cuz you're good at creeping around."

Creepy Karpis's smile grew almost too wide for his face. "Right you are, Liam." He drew out the word "Liam" to make sure Liam knew that he'd learned his name. "I've been creeping all night. I've followed you everywhere. I know everything you know. Now, we talk."

"We won't talk until you bring us Mason!" Tommy shouted.

Creepy Karpis shot Tommy a look so menacing that the kids actually gasped out loud. "You'll talk when I tell you to talk."

Tommy stopped talking.

"Mason is safe at the professor's house with my former associates."

"Former?" Elsa asked.

"I have new associates now." Creepy Karpis spread his arms. "You."

"I'm no one's associate!" Tommy shouted.

Creepy Karpis made a quick motion toward Tommy, which caused Tommy to stumble backward. That brought the gangster great satisfaction. "Might I extend an invitation to the world's first time-traveling gang. No more getaway cars. No more safe houses. No more loose ends or pesky snitches. We travel to the past, pull a job, then come back before anyone's the wiser."

Liam was so confused by this proposal that he could only sputter, "Why . . . why would we . . ."

"Tommy Twinkles would." Creepy Karpis turned toward Tommy. "You'll be my muscle, kid. Let's light up this town."

That small bit of praise completely broke through Tommy's defenses. "Oh!" he said with a silly grin.

"You're not lighting anything up in that time machine," Elsa said. "It's garbage. I'm the only one who knows how to work it."

"Oh, Button," Creepy Karpis said. "Sweet, little Button. You're my getaway driver. I'd never go anywhere without you."

"And I'm never going anywhere with you. So looks like you're stuck."

Quick as lightning, Creepy Karpis grabbed Liam and pulled him to his chest. Liam struggled to escape, but Creepy Karpis had an iron grip. "You're forgetting the last member of the gang," Karpis said. "Liam here is the lemon. When I need some juice from you, all I need to do is squeeze." Creepy Karpis squeezed Liam's chest so tight that he could barely breathe.

"I'm not your lemon," Liam wheezed.

"What?" Creepy Karpis asked, squeezing tighter. "Speak up!"

"I'm your brains," Liam coughed.

That caught Creepy Karpis by surprise. The gangster started cackling, which caused him to loosen his grip enough that Liam could gather a breath.

"You're thinking small," Liam said.

"Yeah? How do you mean, lemon?"

"Why do you want to rob banks when you could take over the world?"

Creepy Karpis cackled again. "Get a load of this kid! Little Napoleon wants to start a war!"

Liam didn't want to start a war. He wanted to cause a distraction. But for the distraction to work, he needed Elsa on board with his plan. He flashed her a quick look and hoped that was enough for her to understand. Hoped it was enough to earn her trust.

"You don't need a war when you know the future," Liam said. "Take John Dillinger. Know when he gets caught? July 22nd, 1934. Got shot trying to escape federal agents. Bet he wishes he knew that was gonna happen. How about Pretty Boy Floyd? Died in a shootout on October 22nd, 1934. Too bad nobody told him that. You know Baby Face Nelson? Shot and killed on November 27th, 1934."

Liam stared at Tommy through the whole speech. Didn't look away once. In addition to distracting Creepy Karpis, Liam was also using this history lesson to make a point to his new friend.

"How about your pals, the Barker Boys? They go down in January 1935. Doc got arrested. Fred wasn't so lucky. And then there's you. Things don't end well for you."

Liam felt Creepy Karpis's grip loosen a bit and heard his breathing change. Good. He had the gangster's full attention.

"You pull a few more jobs, grow your gang, even get away with a train robbery. You become Public Enemy Number One. You get clever. Think you can stay ahead of the FBI by scraping off your fingerprints. That's one of the most painful things you'll ever experience. Also, it doesn't work. You get captured on May 1st, 1936."

"No," Karpis whispered.

"You can keep robbing banks if you want," Liam continued. "But if you ask me, you'd be better off robbing a library."

The room remained silent for a moment. Then, Creepy Karpis spun Liam around and held him at arm's length so he could study him with his dead fish eyes. Liam wanted to turn away, but he met the gaze with a clenched jaw. Finally, Karpis said, "You made that up."

Liam shook his head. "I read it in a book. That one." Liam nodded toward the Thomas Edison book that was still lying on his dad's workbench.

Creepy Karpis glanced over, then smiled when he saw the title: *Man of Genius*. "That about me, huh?" He pushed Liam aside and stepped toward the book.

"NOW!" Liam yelled.

Throughout Liam's speech, Elsa had crept ever so slowly toward the time machine. At Liam's command, she plugged it in.

23
CREEPIER KARPIS

BLURP!

The machine sputtered to life. Creepy Karpis turned with wide eyes, then dove toward Elsa, but he was too late. A purple bolt snaked out of the time machine and zapped his chest.

ZZZZZZZ—

Unlike Mr. and Mrs. Chapman, Creepy Karpis did not quietly disappear into time jail. Maybe it was because the chaos meter had moved to within a half-tick of eleven. Maybe it was Karpis's belief in the machine's power.

—ZZZZAAAA—

Whatever the reason, Karpis was able to fight against the current coursing through his body. For a second, it looked like he might win. He squirmed and writhed and was even able to take a step toward the kids. They backed up.

—AAAAAAA—

The purple electricity grew more intense. Karpis started to flicker, then appeared to s-t-r-r-r-e-e-e-t-c-h like slime. His final act was grabbing the bronze dog statue off the workbench and cocking it back to throw at the kids.

—AAAAAAAP!

With one last surge, the time machine zapped Creepy Karpis into oblivion.

The kids stared for a second, then Tommy started jumping. "HOT DOG!" He ran a lap around the basement punching the air with excitement. "HOT DOG, WE DID IT!" Then, he jumped onto Liam's back, nearly knocking him over. "YOU DID IT! YOU DID IT WITH THE BOOK STUFF!"

"It wasn't the book, it was Google!" Liam exclaimed. "I read it on my dad's phone earlier. I wanted to show you what happens to gangsters."

Elsa smiled. "You finally did the reading."

PUUUUUUUTZ!

The time machine wheezed a cloud of black smoke. Then, it started shaking.

Thunk-thunk-thunk-thunk.

"Wait, why's it doing that?" Liam asked.

"I don't know," Elsa replied.

ZING!

The machine shot a beam of purple light straight to the ceiling.

"WHY'S IT DOING *THAT*?!"

"I DON'T KNOW!"

Tommy picked up the time machine's phone receiver and dialed zero. "Operator! Operator!"

"That's not how you do it!" Elsa shoved Tommy aside and started dialing another number.

"But I heard something," Tommy said. "It was like a voice, or a . . . a . . ."

DING!

The chaos meter struck eleven, causing the basement to erupt into mayhem. Walls appeared to flex in and out. Deep rumbling shook the ground. The purple light beam shooting from the time machine suddenly blasted a wave of energy, knocking the kids to the ground. Then, the beam began to flicker and wave. It looked like a big, purple noodle. It grew thicker and started developing human features. Very creepy features.

"SHUT IT OFF!" Liam screamed. Elsa scrambled toward the fuse box.

Creepy Karpis's face came back first. It glowed brightly on top of the wiggly, purple light noodle. Then, that noodle split into separate beams of light for his legs and arms. Finally, one of those beams grew a hand that held the Sleepy Barkis statue.

Karpis spotted Elsa going for the fuse box, wound up his long, purple arm, and threw the bronze dog as hard as he could.

"ELSA!" Tommy screamed.

Elsa dodged Sleepy at the last second, and the dog ended up smashing into the fuse box.

POP!

Upon impact, an arc of blue electricity exploded from the fuse box, and the basement plunged into darkness. Finally, Creepy Karpis flickered and disappeared.

Liam grabbed a flashlight from his dad's workbench. "Elsa?!"

Elsa was fine. So was Tommy. Liam turned his flashlight toward the time machine and breathed a sigh of relief when he found no Creepy Karpis.

"What's that?" Tommy asked.

Curled around the time machine was a long, black tube. The kids drew closer. The tube started moving.

"SNAAAAKE!" Tommy screamed as he stumbled backward.

Unfortunately, the tube was not a snake. That would have been way, way better than what it turned out to be. The tube stretched and unwound itself until the kids saw something that made them all scream.

"HAND!" Elsa yelled as she jumped back even farther.

It was indeed a hand. A hand with five long fingers. The hand felt around until it grabbed the time machine's power cord and ripped it from the box.

RIIIIIIING!

That set off the chaos meter. It rang at full volume, but the kids barely noticed. They were transfixed by the sight in front of them. The tube used the workbench to pull itself up, revealing its full horror.

RIIIIIIING!

It was Creepy Karpis. The purple light beam was gone, but his long, noodle body remained.

RIIIIIIING!

Karpis snaked his arm to the ground and picked up the chaos meter. He lifted it close to his face and squinted. The meter had finally hit midnight.

RIIIII-

SLAM!

Karpis stopped the ringing by slamming the chaos meter to the ground, smashing it into a million pieces. Then, he turned to the kids.

24
MIDNIGHT

While Creepy Karpis stumbled toward the kids with his noodle legs, a crack began forming on the basement floor. It snaked between Creepy Karpis's feet all the way to the time machine. The earth began to shake.

"Outside! Now!" Elsa screamed as she grabbed the time machine.

The kids took the stairs two at a time. Both Creepy Karpis and the crack followed them. Liam was the last one out the door, so he slammed it behind him.

"Arrrgghh!" A mangled scream told Liam he'd slammed the door on Creepy Karpis's arm.

Elsa used the bungee cord to secure the time machine to the bike trailer with the barrels. "We're going to Mason's house!" she yelled. "Follow me!"

Liam and Tommy hopped on Liam's bike, and they took off.

CRASH!

Behind them, Creepy Karpis burst through the door.

CRACK!

In front of them, giant cracks formed in the street.

The kids pedaled harder. Creepy Karpis tried keeping up but was finding it difficult to run on his new noodle legs, especially with the earthquake going on. He stumbled and wobbled down the sidewalk.

The cracks turned out to be the tougher obstacle. Each crack split open to reveal a deep chasm filled with purple light. The kids swerved back and forth, using every ounce of concentration to avoid falling into the abyss of time and space.

SNAP!

Elsa turned onto Mason's street so hard that a bungee cord snapped, and one of the barrels bounced off the bike trailer.

"No!" Elsa slammed on the brakes, but she couldn't reach the barrel. It rolled toward a crack.

"Got it!" Tommy jumped off of Liam's moving bicycle. He hit the ground, rolled twice, popped to his feet, then tackled the barrel right before it fell into the chasm.

CRAAAACK!

Cracks started surrounding the bikes now, almost as if they were working together to trap the kids. "Go!" Tommy shouted. "I'll catch up!"

Liam and Elsa raced down the street. They managed to keep pace ahead of the cracks, but Elsa started huffing and puffing with the extra weight she was towing. As Liam and Elsa pedaled for their lives, the cracks behind them united into one giant rift. Light from the pit turned the night sky purple. Neighbors stared at the scene with their mouths agape.

One of those neighbors was Mr. Farkas. He stood in the doorway of his garage in boxer shorts, taking pictures with his iPad.

"Mr. Farkas!" Elsa screamed. "Your Tesla! We need the charger!"

Mr. Farkas glanced at the rift approaching his house, then started backing up.

"MR. FARKAS!"

Mr. Farkas retreated back into the house and hit the button to close his garage door.

Nope. No way. Liam wasn't going to let it end like this. He pedaled ahead of Elsa, jumped the curb, cut across the lawn, then sped toward the closing garage. He pictured himself sliding his bike under the garage at full speed like he was on a motorcycle in an action movie. That's not exactly what happened. His attempt to start the slide ended with him flipping over the handlebars. He still rolled under the garage door, just with much less knee and elbow skin than he had a moment earlier.

When the garage door sensed Liam, it opened back up, letting Elsa inside. She tried hitting the brakes, but the parked Tesla did more to stop her momentum than the brakes did.

CRASH!

Mr. Farkas lost his mind when he saw the damage. "AHHHHHHH!"

Elsa unloaded the time machine from her bike trailer. "I need a funnel!"

"MY TESLA!"

"FUNNEL!"

Liam grabbed a funnel from one of the shelves, while Elsa lugged the time machine over to the Tesla charger. She ripped the charger out of the car and jammed it into the hole in the cardboard where the power cord had been. Liam threw Elsa the funnel, then pulled one of the blue barrels from the bike trailer. He glanced back at the street. The giant rift had almost reached the Farkas house. "You sure this is gonna work?" he asked Elsa.

"Yes! And you'd better be sure too!"

Elsa flipped a switch on the time machine, and black smoke started chugging. That was a good sign. The rift raced up the Farkas driveway. That was a bad sign. Elsa dialed the phone, then unscrewed one end of the receiver and shoved the funnel into it. "Pour!" she instructed.

When Liam poured time slime into the funnel, the room immediately got cooler. He glanced back at the rift. It was retreating. "It's working!"

Even better, Tommy arrived with the final barrel of time slime.

"IT'S WORKING!" Liam repeated with a fist pump before starting the second barrel.

Tommy did not share in the enthusiasm. His eyes were wide, and his hair was crazy. He looked like he was trying to say something, but he was breathing too hard to get the words out.

"What is it?!" Elsa asked.

Tommy didn't get to answer because, at that moment, a slithery black arm smacked him across the garage.

25

FARKAS FRACAS

Creepy Karpis ducked his head into the garage and smiled when he saw the time machine. It should go without saying that the smile on his stretched face was the creepiest smile that anyone has ever smiled in the history of smiles. He pushed Liam aside and reached for the time machine.

As soon as Liam stopped pouring time slime, the rift started advancing again. Elsa grabbed Creepy Karpis's arm and pulled it away. "KEEP POURING!"

Liam continued pouring while his friends did their best to keep Creepy Karpis busy. It wasn't easy. The garage was so full of flailing arms and legs that the kids couldn't coordinate their attack, let alone defend themselves. It didn't take long before Creepy Karpis had Elsa wrapped like an anaconda with one arm and Tommy smooshed against the Tesla with the other arm.

With Elsa and Tommy under control, Creepy Karpis snaked his head next to Liam's. "I've got two lemons, and I'm ready to squeeze," he said with a raspy voice. "Stop pouring."

Liam locked eyes with Elsa. She shook her head. Liam kept pouring.

Creepy Karpis flexed his noodle muscles. Tommy and Elsa both sputtered and gasped. "Stop. Pouring," he repeated.

Liam kept pouring.

Creepy Karpis's face turned red. "STOP . . ."

CRACK!

Mr. Farkas smashed Creepy Karpis over the head with a plastic snow shovel. "BACK OFF THE TESLA!"

Just like his son, Mr. Farkas was under the mistaken impression that a smack to the head was all it would take to knock out a gangster. Unfortunately, he would be the second Farkas of the evening to learn the error of his ways. The smack did not knock out Creepy Karpis. But it did make him furious.

Creepy Karpis let go of Tommy and Elsa to unleash his full fury on the man with the shovel. Mr. Farkas was up for the challenge. Protecting his Tesla gave him the strength of ten men. While the Karpis-Farkas fracas raged, the kids joined Liam back at the time machine.

"Last barrel!" Liam called.

Tommy rolled the barrel to Liam, and Elsa helped load it into place. As the final barrel guzzled into the time machine, fog started filling the room. "I can't see!" Tommy panicked.

"That means it's working!" Elsa assured him. "In a few seconds, you'll be back home."

"My head hurts!"

"It'll hurt for a second, then it'll all be over. You won't remember a thing!"

"Won't remember?!"

"Nobody will remember. It'll be like it never happened!"

"Nononono . . ." Tommy moaned.

"We'll remember you!" Liam said.

"But she said . . ."

"Listen to me!" The fog grew so intense that Liam could barely see Tommy's face. "The world will remember you. Do something worth remembering."

As soon as the words left Liam's mouth, he watched Tommy turn to vapor. Then, Liam turned to Elsa. "I want to remember."

"That's not the way it works," Elsa said.

The last of the time slime poured out in glugs. Any second now, it would be gone.

"But you said! Way back at the beginning! You said you knew how to remember!"

"Cccckkkk!" Elsa tried talking, but the words coming out of her mouth sounded like static. Then the fog overtook her.

Liam's head hurt. A lot. He felt dizzy. Darkness started replacing the white fog. But right before everything disappeared, Elsa pushed her face real close to Liam's. Her eyes were crossed.

Liam crossed his eyes too. Then, the world faded away.

CHRISTMAS DAY

Gaaaaaasp!

Liam sucked in a giant breath like he'd just emerged from the ocean. His eyes popped open in a panic. He was back in his bedroom. The alarm clock read 7:01 a.m.

Liam's brain felt like it'd just been dumped into a blender. He tried to remember what kind of crazy dream would have him feeling like this. It took a full minute for his memory to return, but once it did, everything crashed into his mind at once.

"MOM!" Liam screamed as he leaped from his bed. *Oof!* His legs weren't exactly working yet. He wobbled to his feet and tried again. "MOM! DAD!"

"Wha—Oof!"

Liam knocked over his mom when he barreled out of his bedroom.

"YOU'RE BACK!" Liam helped his mom up, hugged her, then jumped up and down.

"What's going on?" Liam's dad asked.

"DAD!" Liam tried repeating the jumping and hugging routine, but his dad put a stop to it.

"This a prank?" Dad asked.

Liam had a goofy smile on his face. "I—I love you."

Liam's mom and dad exchanged a bewildered look. "Um, we love you, too," Mom finally said. "Want me to drive you to school? That garage sale's today, and there are some pretty weird guys . . ."

"It's garage sale day?! Haha!" That set Liam off on another hugging and jumping spree. He ran downstairs, grabbed a banana, then went full Ebenezer Scrooge on Christmas Day when he saw all the weirdos in front of his house.

"Cats are spies! Wahoooo!" Liam danced down the street, hugging every person he recognized. "Ernie! End of Days! MAPSI!"

"This young man looks especially excited to shop at the garage sale today," Mortimer Pitts of Mocha with Morty in the Morning reported when Liam walked into his shot.

"IT'S GARAGE SALE DAY!" Liam yelled before performing a dance for the camera so uncoordinated that it was destined to headline news blooper videos for years to come.

Finally, Liam reached Elsa at the bus stop. She glanced at him out of the corner of her eye like she was trying to figure out whether or not he remembered the adventure. "You're early," she said.

Liam responded the same way he'd responded all morning: with a giant hug. "We did it!"

"OK, OK," Elsa pushed Liam away but couldn't keep a smile from creeping across her face. "Everything normal at your house?"

Screeeeech.

Before Liam could answer, the school bus pulled up. The door opened, and Mrs. Kessling just about fell out of her seat when she saw her archnemesis waiting for her.

"You see something new every day," she muttered.

• • •

The next day, Ms. Sosa's class sat awkwardly while Mason Farkas spun a bicycle wheel adorned with twenty spoons.

Clinkclinkclinkclink-Thud!

The wheel tipped off of Mason's finger and crashed to the ground. "So in conclusion," Mason said over the noise of clattering spoons, "that's how Nikola Tesla invented the world's greatest automobile. Thank you."

"Thank you, Mason," Ms. Sosa said. "I do feel like I need to tell the rest of the class that Nikola Tesla did not invent the Tesla automobile—a fact Mr. Farkas might have learned had he actually read his book."

Mason walked back to his seat with a smug look on his face.

"Now, for the final presentation of the day," Ms. Sosa said. "Liam Chapman."

Liam walked to the front of the classroom lugging a cardboard box long enough to hold a piano keyboard. A power cord snaked out of the box and bounced on the ground behind him as he walked. Liam's heart pounded. He never got nervous for these reports, but today was different.

Liam cleared his throat. "Today, I'm going to tell you about Thomas Edison. Thomas was born on April 4th, 1922. We don't know his parents' names. We don't know where he grew up or if he had siblings or what classes he liked in school. But we do know he was a good friend. And we know he grew up to be a good man. How do we know that, you ask?"

Neither Ms. Sosa nor anyone in the class had asked that, but Liam produced the evidence anyway. He fumbled through his pocket and pulled out a folded sheet of paper. "This is an, um, obituary. That's a thing they write in newspapers when people die." His voice cracked a little. "It's from the *Bellevue Register*, which is a newspaper in Ohio. You can find it on their website if you subscribe. I think it's $2.99 for the first month."

Liam cleared his throat and read. "Thomas Gerard Edison passed away peacefully on May 10th, 2008, surrounded by family and friends. Edison was a World War II veteran who served in the Pacific Theater. He was awarded a Silver Star for his bravery in battle." Liam looked up just long enough to give Elsa a quivery smile. She responded with her own quivery smile.

"After the war, Thomas returned to Bellevue to marry the love of his life, Beatrice. He served faithfully on the Bellevue Police Force until he retired in 1985. Thomas was a valued member of the community in retirement. He organized the Mahoning Valley Birdwatching Club in 1987 and led efforts to build the Front Street Library in 1991."

Liam fumbled in his pocket again. "Um, I found a picture of the Front Street Library. It looks kind of like our spaceship library. See?" Liam held up the picture. "Anyways, the rest of the obituary talks about his kids and grandkids. He had a lot of them, and it sounds like they were all there when he died, which is nice."

Liam yawned, which was an interesting technique for keeping himself from crying in front of the class. Then, he plugged in the power cord from the piano keyboard box he'd brought. "This is a little project to honor the life of Thomas Edison." Liam opened the box with a flourish to reveal a tangled strand of Christmas lights. "It's really hard to spell stuff with Christmas lights, but that's supposed to say, 'Tommy Twinkles.' I thought that would be nice for him. He always wanted to see his name in lights."

Elsa applauded loudly. The rest of the class followed along, but it was more of a confused applause than anything else. When the clapping died down, Ms. Sosa spoke up.

"Thank you, Liam. I think there may have been some confusion about the assignment. However, the real Thomas Edison did invent the light bulb, so the Christmas lights were appropriate I suppose."

Liam smiled and wiped away a tear. "With all due respect, Ms. Sosa, you've got the wrong Thomas Edison."

ONE MORE THING!

You know how superhero movies have after-credits scenes? This book has one, too! Check it out after the About the Author section.

MEET THE CAST

Did you know that several characters in this book are real-life people from history? Here are their stories.

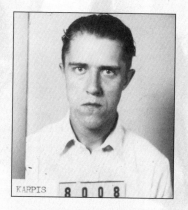

KARPIS 8008

ALVIN KARPIS

Alvin Karpis never became as famous as criminals like Al Capone or John Dillinger, but he didn't mind. Unlike many of the big-name crooks of his time, Karpis wasn't flashy or loud. This low profile helped him pull off fifteen bank robberies, three jail breaks, and two kidnappings.

OLD CREEPY

Alvin Karpis went by several nicknames. People called him "Slim" because he was so thin and "Chi" because he loved the city of Chicago. But the nickname that really stuck was "Old Creepy." Most people assumed the nickname came from his sinister smile and long, scary face, but Karpis claimed that he'd earned the name because he was so good at creeping around and avoiding law enforcement.

THE LAST TRAIN ROBBERY

On November 7th, 1935, Karpis and his gang pulled off the last successful train robbery in American history. In the small town of Garrettsville,

Ohio, Karpis ambushed a train carrying $45,650 to pay factory workers. In today's money, that's over $1 million. Karpis took the loot to a waiting airplane and flew to Arkansas, making him the first criminal to get away by air.

THE BARKER BOYS

If Alvin Karpis was the brains behind the Karpis-Barker gang, the Barker brothers were the muscle. The "Bloody Barkers" were never afraid to get their hands dirty as the gang terrorized towns throughout the Midwest.

Fred Barker

A WASTED LIFE

Karpis tried outwitting police by meticulously planning every job, moving around the country, and even paying a doctor to remove his fingerprints. None of it mattered. The FBI arrested him on May 1st, 1936. Karpis then spent twenty-five years in the infamous Alcatraz prison, earning the record for longest stay on the island. Karpis admitted a few years before his death that crime had led to a "wasted life."

PRISON PALS

Karpis met Fred Barker (aka "Bowl Cut" Barker) in the Kansas State Penitentiary. The two eventually became cellmates and best buddies. One of their first bonding activities after getting out of jail was robbing a bank in Tulsa, Oklahoma. They drove away with $7,000, dropping roofing tacks behind their getaway car to keep the police from following them.

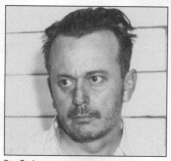

Doc Barker

Ma Barker

TEAM UP

A year later, big brother Arthur "Doc" Barker (aka "Mustache" Barker) got out of prison and joined the gang. Together, they went on a bank-robbing spree before deciding they could make more money by kidnapping wealthy businessmen. The Karpis-Barker gang was so successful that John Dillinger himself suggested that their gangs should team up.

MA

Legend has it that the real leader of the Karpis-Barker gang was actually Fred and Doc Barker's mom. Although we now understand that Kate "Ma" Barker wasn't the criminal mastermind that rumors built her up to be, she did live with the gang until the day she died. Ma Barker looked after the criminals, and in return, the criminals took care of her.

THOMAS EDISON

Tommy Twinkles is a fictional character, but he gets his own section here because his attitude toward gangsters comes from real life. For several years in the 1930s, gangsters actually became heroes to many Americans. Why?

DEPRESSION

During the Great Depression years of the early 1930s, the economy was so bad that banks began failing, losing all the hard-earned money people had deposited into them. Some Americans cheered gangsters who robbed banks because they felt that bankers were the real bad guys.

PUBLIC ENEMIES

Gangsters lost popularity as they started hurting more and more innocent people. Authorities took advantage of this attitude shift by enlisting everyday people to help them track down these "public enemies" through things like announcement at the start of movies. Before every movie, audiences were instructed to look left and right because a notorious gangster might be sitting in their row.

J. Edgar Hoover

G-MEN

By the time Alvin Karpis got caught, his type was no longer idolized. The man who arrested him—J. Edgar Hoover— represented a new type of American hero. Hoover had just formed the FBI, an elite squad of crime fighters that gangsters called the "G-Men" (government men). By the end of the 1930s, these G-Men were so popular that it was harder to get into the FBI than an elite Ivy League college.

Special thanks to Julie A. Thompson and her book The Hunt for the Last Public Enemy in Northeastern Ohio *for the facts found in this section.*

ABOUT DUSTIN BRADY

Dustin Brady writes books for kids who think they hate reading. His *Trapped in a Video Game* series has sold over two million copies because—as it turns out—there are a lot of kids who think they hate reading. Dustin loves *Tetris*, pinball, trick shot videos, and many other silly pastimes that he calls "book research" even though they very much don't seem like book research. He lives in Cleveland, Ohio, with his wife, three kids, and a small dog named Nugget. Dustin honestly can't believe he gets to do this for a living.

ABOUT DAVE BARDIN

Dave Bardin is a freelance illustrator and animator residing in Southern California. When Dave drew his very first comic book at the age of nine, he knew he had found what he wanted to do for the rest of his life. As a freelance artist for the last nine years, Dave has had the opportunity to work on a variety of creative projects with some of the biggest names in media. These projects include comic books, video games, board games, animation, commercials, music videos, and television. When Dave isn't at the drawing board, he can be found riding his bike down by the beach, going on random driving adventures with his very cool wife, and spending time with his friends and family.

AFTER-CREDITS SCENE

"This isn't gonna work," Elsa declared as she tightened one final screw.

"Not with that attitude, it won't!" Liam replied.

Elsa stepped back to admire her handiwork. She'd just reassembled the time machine in Professor Snellenburg's cellar, and it looked ten times more professional than Liam's attempt. Before she plugged it in, she turned to Liam. "If we mess this up, we're on our own. None of the time slime came back."

"Relax," Liam said. "We won't do anything crazy."

Elsa sighed and powered up the time machine. The box gurgled for a second, but didn't do much else.

"OK," Liam continued. "Now dial zero."

"I thought you were gonna do the honors."

"I don't know how to dial these old phones."

Elsa rolled her eyes and dialed zero. She held the receiver to her ear. "Nothing."

"Tommy heard the voice after he asked for the operator. Maybe you've got to do that."

"No one's on the line!"

"Just do it!"

"Operator," Elsa said flatly.

"Like you mean it!"

"You do it!"

A sudden burst of static hissed over the phone. Elsa threw the receiver down like it'd just turned into a snake. When the hissing stopped, she gingerly picked it up again. "Um, hello?"

"Elsa?" a voice crackled from the receiver.

The kids stopped breathing.

"Is that my little button?" the voice asked.

All the color drained from Elsa's face. "Grandpa?"

LOOK FOR THESE BOOKS BY DUSTIN BRADY